SUCH GREAT HEIGHTS

SUCH GREAT
HEIGHTS

Maria Tyler

iUniverse, Inc.
Bloomington

Such Great Heights

iUniverse books may be ordered through booksellers or by contacting:

iUniverse
1663 Liberty Drive
Bloomington, IN 47403
www.iuniverse.com
1-800-Authors (1-800-288-4677)

ISBN: 978-1-4502-9123-1 (sc)
ISBN: 978-1-4502-9125-5 (hc)
ISBN: 978-1-4502-9124-8 (e)

Printed in the United States of America

iUniverse rev. date: 08/29/2011

A mother's love for her child is like nothing else in the world. It knows no law, no pity, it dares all things, and crushes down remorselessly all that stands in its path.

-Agatha Christie-

TABLE OF CONTENTS

CHAPTER 1

I pulled into the underground employee parking garage exactly five minutes before my day started. It was dark, and like any underground parking my foot steps echoed. I explained to the parking attendant that it was my first day and did not yet receive my parking pass. He made me sign my name in the registry and after doing so I grabbed my purse and bags from the floor to make my way to the exit leading outside of the building. The parking attendant eyed my black Mercedes S-Class with an envious look the whole time, therefore *I* was eyeing the parking attendant and not for the reasons he thought. Though I considered my self a good looking woman, men often had a tendency toward my car than me. I pushed my long straight black hair over my shoulders, and with one more warning glare toward 'Mr. McStaresalot's' direction. I entered the exit door, and went around to the front of the grey brick and glass building.

Breathe in…breathe out…okay… here goes nothing. I encouraged myself mentally.

Before I opened one of the glass doors I looked up, and basked in the gold-metal lettering that was hovering about twenty feet above my head.

New York Police Department – Precinct #57
As I stepped through the gold and glass doors a shiver of anticipation and nervousness shot through my body. I took that as a good sign of things to come.

I hoped!

I walked fully inside, and noticed the big black signs hanging from the ceiling directing people where to go. The environment was very formal, the floors where grey ceramic, and the walls a dull white, though the reception area looked quite elegant with its mahogany desk, and the big carving behind it stating the precinct number. I looked for the sign leading to my new office following them through narrow corridors, and when I found it, I couldn't help the wide smile spreading across my face.

Dr. B. Rivers, Ph.D., Psychologist...*dad would have been so proud of me!* I thought.

I looked around the area, and noticed the wide windows, the beige and white walls littered with Wanted posters, the whiteboards, and the numerous computers, and television screens to the left. Two sets of stairs flanked the left wall, leading to god knows where. There were a bunch of cubicles off to the side by the windows right in front of my office, there was also an office toward the back with white vertical blinds drawn shut just like mine, and a hallway that more than likely lead to the holding cells, and interrogation rooms, I imagined.

I unlocked my door, and couldn't believe the sight before me. Fucking hell!

Now, I don't curse a lot, but that moment was a good time to start. The former Doctor decided he was in too much of a hurry to get the fuck out of here to clean up the god damn place.

Pardon my French!

Papers and files were scattered all over the desk, the coffee table, and even the floor. The drawers of the file cabinet were almost all open, and by looking closer, most of them were empty.

This was going to take me hours...(Sigh)...well there was no time to just stand around!

That was how I spent my morning. Sitting on the floor with my shoes off, sorting through all that crap, filling them back in the cabinet, and cleaning this dump. At least it was going to look great; the walls were light beige like the outside corridors, I had a nice black leather chair and sofa on the right wall with a beautiful mahogany coffee table. My desk, also mahogany, was in an angle on the left side facing the door, and bonus…I had my own private bathroom. Woohoo!

I stood to dump a few files on my desk, and spotted the bags I had brought with me sitting there. Opening one, I took out a picture frame, and placed it on my desk so it would face me. My beautiful little girl, Hayley, was the spitting image of me, dark emerald green eyes, pouty lips, and quite a personality to match my own. Only her hair, she had her father's hair, was an ashy blond, and mine were pitch black.

I heard a knock at the door that startled me, almost making me launch Hayley's frame right up in the air.

"Come in," I looked up to see who my visitor was; realizing with relief that he was no stranger to me.

"Good morning Dr. Rivers, how…Oh I'm so sorry about this," he said with a remorseful gesture toward the mess. "Dr. Lewis was not very happy with us when he left, and I've been meaning to get someone to clean…"

"Please Captain Broadway, it's alright. It gives me a chance to sort, and file everything my self like I want it to be, and reading them through. It's no problem at all," I said trying to soothe is concern, and putting the frame in its new spot on my desk.

Captain Broadway was a large man, a little balding on top of his head with salt, and pepper hair all the way around, and piercing black eyes. I had no doubt he must have been a very handsome man back in the day, but unfortunately, now around his mid-fifties, he looked tired, and worn out. Being in charge of the Crisis Negotiations Team (CNT) or if you prefer Hostage Negotiations Team must have had a toll on him.

The 57th Precinct is mostly residential area in Harlem. Unfortunately the crime rate was pretty high, and my job was to provide trauma debriefing, counseling, and evaluation of Captain Broadway's team when needed after major incidences, events, and crisis or during times of personal needs, and I also had to evaluate the investigative personnel for psychological fitness for specialized assignments. So, yeah, I did have my work cut out for me, and I *loved* it.

The Captain cleared his throat to get my attention again. "I was just passing by to tell you that we'll be having a staff meeting in thirty minutes in the boardroom 404. I would like to introduce you, and you can say a little something to the gang if you need too. Is that alright?"

"That's perfectly fine Capt…" he cut me off by raising his right hand.

"Please, call me Ed."

"Alright, well its fine…Ed, and I'll be there, thank you," I laughed.

He chuckled, and left me to my cleaning again. Oh crap on a cracker… now I had to face the whole team. Great, just fabu-freaking-less.

Just then I heard the sound of my favorite Nickelback song coming from my purse. I dove in, almost emptying the contents on the desk to grab my cell before who ever it was hung up.

"Hello?"

"Good morning, I would like to speak to Miss Belladonna Rivers?"

"Yes, that's me. How can I help you?" I said, a little weary. I didn't recognize the voice.

"My name is John Fitz from the Department of Public Safety in Los Angeles," he stopped talking as if letting me take in the introduction, and my heart stopped as I realized what subject he wanted to discuss. My throat dried up, my hands clamed up, and I fell into my chair with tears forming in my eyes.

"Yes," was all I was able to conjure up.

"I'm calling you in regards of Mr. Brian Jamieson. His parole hearing went very well, and the parole board has granted him his release under probation for two years," he spoke in a very calm voice, and a little too much as a matter of fact for my taste.

"Since you have decided not to voice your opinion on the matter of his parole hearing I am in the obligation of informing you that his release date is set for a week from yesterday. We would like to inform you also that your restraining order has not been removed. Mr. Jamieson is still under the restriction to approach you, and your daughter unless he contacts you through your lawyer first," Mr. Fitz added.

"Okay, thank you," and I hung up effectively cutting off his next words. I was in total shock. I don't know how long I sat staring at my phone trying to swallow what I had just learned. I knew his parole hearing was coming, but never in a millions years had I thought he would be granted. If I would have had a single doubt I would have objected. I would have with all my might. I snapped out of it when loud voices came to me from the corridor, and when I looked at the clock, crap…my meeting.

Pull yourself together B, staff meeting in ten minutes!

I threw my phone back in my purse, and started breathing in, and out slowly trying to calm my self. I could do this, I knew I could. It had been a year since I gathered up enough courage to divorce him, and report him to local authority, but it still had an affect on me in more ways than one. As a psychologist, I have been able to not crumble, and fall on my knees, but it's not like a light switch I could turn on, and off…the memories of his abuse still lingered in the back of my mind.

CHAPTER 2

"Hey Collin, if you think the car's hot, wait until you see its owner," Jeffrey, the parking attendant, bellowed at the top of his lungs.

I had parked my blue Ducati next to a kick ass black Mercedes. I had no idea who the hell drove it, but dude had some serious balls driving that thing around in Harlem. Shaking my head in awe, I removed my helmet, and ran my fingers through my short brown hair to tame the mess the helmet created. I turned around to see Jeffrey looking at me, and smiled an all knowing smile. I just smiled back, and started to walk away when he called on me again almost as loud as before.

"Hey…by the way I call dibs dude, so back off pretty-boy," he warned me. Well, I guessed the owner was a woman; she had taste that's for sure.

"You don't even know if she's single, and you're already staking claim on her?" I asked "Well by all means good luck with that," I added not waiting for him to answer.

"You'll be sorry, Haywood. If I was you, and not stuck in this booth I'd be all over this chick, ASAP."

"Yeah Jeff, because you're opinion means so much to me. Anyway, I have a staff meeting, and an actual job to get to, so I'll leave you to dream about that in your little box," I said tapping my knuckles on the booth window. He nodded his head glaring at me, and we said our goodbyes before making my way inside.

I dropped my helmet on my desk before putting my leather coat on the back of my chair, and heard Captain Broadway talking to someone. I looked on my right, and noticed the psychologist's office door open, and the Captain standing against the frame. Ah, the new Doc was here. I still hadn't heard who he was, but I fucking hoped he was better than old Lewis, guy was getting senile. It was about time they made him retire.

I booted my computer, and immersed my self in the ever growing pile of paper work, and reports on my desk, not really paying attention to my surrounding when a hand clapped on my back.

"Are you coming or not?" Riley said.

"Ugh? What…" I looked at my watch and…fuck already!

"Staff meeting, let's go or you'll get your balls cut off by Broadway again."

Riley Price was my best friend, and partner in crime. If you need to pull a prank he's the first person you should call. He's not very inconspicuous with his six foot height and broad shoulders but he can be a great asset to any prank you want to commit.

"Yeah go ahead, I'll be right there."

I closed up my files, and as I got closer to the boardroom, I heard the buzz of voices coming from everyone already there, but one in particular stirred me in ways I couldn't really believe. I picked up my pace, and when I rounded the corner…complete, and utter brain wipe.

Oh my God…HALLE-FUCKING-LUJAH!

I'm talking bells chiming, angels singing, harps being plucked-type shit here people. Was I dead? Because that was the only reason this…Angel could have been standing no more than ten feet from me. Her black hair hung straight all the way to the middle of her back, her eyes were a deep emerald green, and her lips…as a gentleman I'll keep my thoughts to my self. This woman was the epitome of beauty, and it took too much damn concentration for me to remember how to walk properly.

Must…not…fall.

My entrance must not have been as smooth as I thought because I noticed her tilt her head slightly in my direction; her eyes silently followed me as I went to take a seat. So I slowly walked over to Riley's side, and slumped my six foot two frame in the very uncomfortable plastic chair while trying to be nonchalant about it, and act like I didn't see her looking at me, but my insides were doing back flips, and my mind was doing imaginary fist pumps, and shit.

As I ran my fingers through my hair again, nervously this time, I let my eyes run over her form when I was sure she wasn't looking my way anymore and…stupid…fucking …move! Her black skirt clung to her curves like a second skin, and the red high heels made her legs look miles long. When her hand went into her hair, her blazer opened effectively making her white blouse tightened on her chest, and I know the polite thing to do was not stare but motherfuck…

Well hello Angel! Jeff wasn't kidding if she's the owner of the Benz…holy shit! I thought.

When I finally looked into her eyes, it was like…like everything I had ever known before this moment was wrong, and unimportant, and useless and….yeah. I felt like she was staring into my soul, and asking me questions, that unlike anyone else, I would have gladly answered. That fact startled me a little, but there was no denying what this woman, this stranger, was doing to my mind…or to my body if I was being honest. When I noticed her gaze turned to me again, and her beautiful green eyes darken to an almost pitch black, I couldn't keep the smile off of my face when I quickly looked away.

Did she want me too? If there was a God, and if I hadn't pissed him off too much, then please let the answer be yes!

I knew I was officially in trouble when she pulled her full bottom lip into her mouth, and my ass moaned! Yeah, this woman had no effect on me whatsoever.

Sarcasm duly noted.

"Good morning everyone, please find your seats, and we'll begin," the Captain said, and the unnamed beauty stood next to Captain Broadway while the rest of the staff sat down. Riley kept nudging my elbow, and wiggling his eyebrows at me, but I couldn't take my eyes off of her.

"*Detective Price*, please pay attention," Riley stopped his childish poking, and looked at the table with the hint of a smile still on his lips. He must have noticed my reaction. Shit, he'll never let this go!

"Thank you," the Captain continued, "I would like to start off by introducing our newest addition to our family. She has completed two years of graduate work, consisting of sixty graduate semester credits in psychology, doctoral degree in counseling, forensic, clinical health,, and neuropsychology; plus two years of full time experience from The Metropolitan Detention Center in Los Angeles under the supervision of her superior. She also completed her American Psychological Association doctoral program in professional psychology. Please welcome to our team Doctor Belladonna Rivers," he stated, motioning her to take over.

Damn, she's probably smarter than you asshole! My inner voice ridiculed me.

I shut off that little part of my brain, and joined everybody else as we clapped, and by the look on the guy's faces, I could only guess the cat calls, and whistles going off in their heads. God knows I was doing it myself. When the noise died down, she stood in front of the room, and looking as confident as she could ever be in front of a bunch of uncivilized men, she spoke to us.

"Thank you Captain Broadway," she said in a soft but firm voice, "I look forward to meeting you all personally. Dr. Lewis has not left me with very much information on who he was seeing at the moment, so I would appreciate it very much if you could all work with me for the next few weeks until I'm done making my own assessment. I will contact your supervisors, and make an appointment for each one of you for the following week, I would be grateful if you could please respect your scheduled time, if you can of course. Thank you," she smiled, and stepped out of the boardroom almost immediately to my utter disappointment.

What? No…well I guessed I'll be seeing her around, I did have a pretty good view of her office from my desk!

I did a little mental tap dance at that realization, and concentrated on what Captain Broadway was saying. The meeting went on as usual, who caught who, what happened to so and so, and who's on the wanted list etc. I stood when we were done, and headed for my ever growing pile of paper work again when Captain Broadway stopped me.

"Detective Haywood, can you step in my office please?" he asked, well actually it sounded more like a demand than a request.

I groaned internally…what now?

"Sure boss," I followed him, and when I passed in front of *her* office I quickly glanced inside. She was sitting on the floor, shoes off; sorting through a huge pile of papers and folders with…fuck me…black framed reading glasses on the tip of her nose.

Damn, what was with her that made me so fucking incoherent? I was acting like a horny thirteen year old. *Focus*, I had to focus. I had a job to do, and it wasn't some chick that was going to fuck it all up. I worked to god damn hard to where I was.

As if feeling she was being watched her head snapped up, and she looked directly at me. She smiled slightly showing a small dimple on the right side of her mouth, but I hadn't really expected to get caught, and I quickly turned to continue toward Ed's office like nothing happened. My ass wasn't even an inch from the chair when the door closed abruptly.

"Haywood, I want to make something very clear with you, so get your head out of your ass, and listen to *me*," he said in a stern voice. Shit. He was standing behind his huge wooden desk, both hands on it, and looking like he wanted to punch me.

"Wow, what happened to Detective Haywood boss?" I said, realizing too late that maybe it wasn't the time for my smart ass to comment; I mentally slapped myself at my verbal diarrhea.

Filter dude! Don't forget to filter between your brain, and mouth. I reminded myself.

"Don't fucking start with me, Collin. Now I am asking this politely so please keep this conversation in mind when you meet with Doctor Rivers. She came highly recommended from her former employer, and professors, don't be an ass, and cooperate with whatever she says. I know the past events have been…" he took a second to search for the proper words, "… hard on you, and I understand it can't be easy to loose a victim on the job but she can help you. Understood?"

"Yes Sir!" I tried to hide my grimace, and did an army style salute, got up, and walked out to my desk a little…okay *really* fucking irritated.

CHAPTER 3

The meeting went well, personally the introduction was a bit much but hey, what can I do. I said what I had to say, and got the hell out of there before that man knocked me on my butt. Oh dear lord I've never seen a face like that!

When I got to the boardroom Ed motioned me over, and introduced me to Captain Moore from the Special Victims Unit. We continued to talk for a while longer until time seemed to all but stop, and my jaw detached from my face when the sexiest, and most drop dead gorgeous man I had ever seen in *all* of my twenty-nine years walked into the room. I swear it was like I was in a movie.

The lights around us dimmed, and a bright spotlight landed on him as his long legs moved in a strong, slow stride. He walked over to a chair next to a big burly guy, and across from where I stood, and my eyes greedily took in the feast before me; brown hair, piercing blue eyes, impeccable white skin, tall, and broad shoulders. I watched as the muscles of his arms moved within the confines of his white t-shirt, and damn near bit my tongue off as he looked up at me. Oh my hot… wow…I'm surprised I was able to do my little speech with him still looking at me.

But then all the magic dissipated when he walked in front of my office, and looked at me sitting on the floor. I tried to give him a polite smile, but I just saw him frown, and abruptly turn around, and walk strait into the Captain's office, the door slamming right after him.

Who in hell did he think he was? Oh that was not going to go down with me.

I continued my work, and paid no attention to him for the remainder of the day…and the next day…and even Wednesday, but when Thursday came around I wanted to scream. It was already hard enough trying to ignore his beautiful blue eyes, but now I had to stare right into them, and assess his mental state. I had other things on my mind than to deal with his temperament, like Brian's…okay not going there.

Crap on a cracker, what was I going to do?

I was reading his file while I was waiting for him to come for his appointment, and damn, the guy had been suspended a total of two months in the last year for bad conduct toward a superior. He had at least a dozen written warnings to his file but the weirdest thing was after the last year, there was absolutely nothing, nada, zip. I knew he'd been here for two and half years because a copy of his employee record is in this file, so why did I only have the last year, what happened that changed his behavior so much?

Knock, knock.

"Come in," I spoke louder than usual to make sure whoever it was heard me, and when *he* came in I almost regretted it. I stood up, and spoke to him with the politeness, and courtesy I give to any of my patients.

"Good morning Detective Haywood, please make your self comfortable," I smiled brightly, and I extended my hand toward the sofa, but instead he didn't even acknowledge me, and sat in front of my desk.

Okaaayyyy…

"Look Doc…I don't have all day, and I'm sort of in a hurry here so question me, and get this over with *please*," he said harshly.

Hold on…what? Oh I don't think so buddy, don't push me asshole! I thought to myself. He may be hot, and beautiful, and I wanted to suck on his bottom lip, but he didn't have the right to speak to me that way.

Okay, breathe in, breathe out. Repeat.

"Detective Haywood, I have been allowed an hour with you by your Captain, and I do intend on using that hour," I said as politely as I could, "Now if you have a prior engagement you should have said so in the first place *before* he confirmed the time with me," I let a small frustrated sigh escape me; it really wasn't a good idea to just blow up in his face.

"Fine," he crossed his arms on his chest childishly, and waited for me to go on. I sat on my chair, pulled his file in front of me, and began.

We went through all my normal testing, and in crude terms the results were quite unusual. I gave him an attitude test, which I now can say he's definitely an ass, the personality test show's he has none or at least he hides it pretty well, and his neuropsychological test shows his neurocognitive functioning are not impaired by any injury or illness he may have had, though I was about to change that.

The whole time, his answers were short, and to the point, he kept glaring at me, and tapping his foot on the floor or his fingers on the arm rest of the chair. I was about to slap him by the time I got to my real question.

"Detective Haywood, you have been here for nearly three years, why don't I have anything on you before the past year?" I asked.

"I don't know," he kept his gaze on the back of the frame with Hayley's picture sitting on my desk, and rolled his eyes.

Mother…Breathe, he's an ass, he's an ass, he's an …I repeated in my head over and over, trying to control myself.

"Did something happen to you?" I knew I was probably walking on egg shells, so I treaded carefully; this guy seemed like a time bomb ready to blow up. To my surprise he growled, and for the first time in an hour his face showed expression, and he spoke louder than before.

"Look, I have nothing else to say to you. Now I have a job to go back too, so if you're done, I'll be on my way."

Okay! That was it. Son of a mother of Mary he had pushed me too far, and my temper stepped in front of my common sense, and my courtesy walked out the door.

I stood up, and leaned on my desk with both hands, "Look here, *Haywood*. I have no idea what the hell crawled up your ass, and died. The glaring, and impatient tapping was one thing but come on, growling, and eye rolling? I don't know what the hell your problem with me is, but either way I refuse to just sit here, and allow you to disrespect me anymore today."

"This is my first week, I just met you, and have done absolutely nothing to you, so whatever your damn drama with me is I highly advise you to leave that shit at home, and at least pretend to be professional while in my office because like it or not you're going to be stuck with me one hour a week so either man the hell up, and deal with it or I will hop my happy ass out of here, and request you take a much needed break...again."

Ass!

I just added that last part in my head for good measure. Seriously? Hot or not, it did not give him the right to be such a prick to me.

"And by the way, the fact that you have me swearing, and it's not even ten o'clock yet bodes extremely well on that *oh so lovely* personality of yours," I added. His knuckles tightened around the arm rest of the chair, and I watched as his baby blue eyes narrowed into slits, his lips pursed, and his perfect pecks rose, and fell with each breath he took. But what surprised me the most was when the corner of his mouth twitched a little.

Ugh!

"Look, Doctor Riv..."

"Save it, and get out," I said pointing at the door. I was so not in the mood for his excuses.

"Fine," he mumbled between clenched teeth, and got up to walk quickly to the door closing it behind him a little more roughly than necessary. His movement made the air around him move, and his scent hit me like a ton of bricks. He didn't smell like cologne, but more like soap, mints and just...manly. I shook my head trying to clear the fog his scent created.

"Thank you God," I breathed, and sat back in my comfortable leather chair, letting the silence calm me. I smiled to myself in pride replaying our first of what I was sure would be many arguments.

CHAPTER 4

G od must have it out for me. That was the only excuse I could come up with because this was some messed up shit right there. What the hell was I going to do? I could not, would not go through that shit again. I did it with Dr. Lewis, and it didn't fucking help.

The obvious thing for me to do was to keep a safe, professional distance, and to stay the hell away from Belladonna Rivers as much as humanly possible because if what I experienced on Monday was any indication whatsoever of what I could possibly feel for her in the future; I was as good as fucked.

Okay, so stay away from the hot Doctor, and keep her away from me. That shouldn't be too hard, after all Riley doesn't call me Collin Douchewood behind my back for nothing.

Jerk.

With my game plan etched in stone, I marched my way over to the most beautiful creature's office that these eyes had ever seen, and turned my dickhead powers on full force. When I snapped at her the first time, the fierce gaze in her eyes sent a fucking chill through my body.

Oh, man she's no kitten. I thought when I saw that spark in her eyes.

I tried to keep things brief, but still polite, and boy was it hard. Her line of questioning was obviously already planned, but when she asked why I hadn't been here before the last year I snapped. I didn't want to go through that again. I had managed to keep that part of my life in the back of my mind, and I was in no way going there again. But then she stood up emerald green eyes blazing, I felt my resolve disintegrate.

Never have I *ever* had someone call my ass out that way, not even Riley…not even my *mother*. Call me spoiled if you want but it's true. People just didn't do it, and when she did, it was like I went into some sort of parallel universe, and I…liked it. I was impressed as all hell by her bravado, and knew that I was right when I saw that fire in her eyes at the beginning of our session. Belladonna Rivers was definitely no kitten… and I was screwed. How in hell could I stay away from someone that I was impressed with, admired her confidence, and was incredibly turned on by? Although due to my earlier actions, it's pretty safe to say that I was on her shit list.

That's what I wanted right? Yes, I wanted her to like me just enough to tolerate an hour a week with me, and that was it. Of course because of my shit induced attitude, she had requested exactly that. Fuck!

Sitting at my desk with my head in my hands, I was trying to come to terms that this vixen of a woman was eventually going to make me spill my guts out, and fuck me…she was already making me want to march back in there, get on my knees, and apologize.

The day went by painfully slowly. Belladonna didn't come out of her office at all, except around five o'clock with her bags in hand. I was already getting up grabbing my helmet after slipping into my coat. She locked her office, and without even throwing a glance my way she headed for the parking lot. I followed behind her, not too close, god knows I was already in her little black book; you know…didn't want to aggravate her even more so she could clinically call my ass insane, and send me to the nut house. She got to her car, and just before she closed the door I passed in front of her Mercedes.

"Have a good evening Doctor Rivers," I said politely, with a small smile.

"B," she said in a voice so low I wasn't sure I heard her. I stopped.

"Excuse me?" I said.

"Call me B. I'm not very comfortable with Doctor, makes me feel like I'm fifty instead of twenty nine," she explained, "and you too, see you tomorrow," she was polite, but her eyes told me she was still beyond pissed at me.

"Alright…see you tomorrow," I replied just before she closed her door. I marched to my bike that was parked next to her passenger side, settled my self, and took off before she did to get dinner on my way home. The grocery store was about two blocks from my house, and there was a little Thailand food counter inside. My sister, who lived with me, was a total addict to it. So I got off the bike, and made my way toward it. After ordering our food, I leaned my back against the counter, and looked around the store. I loved to people watch, but at that moment when my eyes fell on a little patch of blond hair, my stomach clenched, and my hands balled into fists. I was momentarily taken out of my dark thoughts when I saw someone crashed their cart into the one the little girl was next to. I jerked involuntarily, but held my self back. The little girl was fine, her mother…that's when I realized I had not even noticed her mother before this moment. I couldn't believe it, it was Belladonna. I heard the other woman speak to her.

"Would you watch where you're going?" The bitch snapped loudly enough to be heard over the noises of the store.

"Watch where *I'm*…" B answered but stopped for a few seconds. Her back was to me, and I couldn't see her face. "Oh my God that's a brilliant idea! Thank you! Let's go sweetie," she continued, and took the little girl's hand to lead her away.

"Excuse me!" The other woman replied, clearly offended. She began ranting in a pitch so high I doubt dogs could even bear it. B just continued making her way to the cash registers not bothering with the womans' screeching.

"Here you go sir." A teenager with so many holes in his face I couldn't even count them all, handed me the boxes, and with some inner pep speech I willed my legs to move toward the cash registers. Without even thinking I stood behind B with the little blond girl.

"Some people just don't know courtesy huh?" I said. She spun around, almost as if expecting the other woman to come scream at her some more.

"Detective Haywood…hum…hi!" she said, surprised.

"Please, call me Collin, Detective is only for the criminals," I chuckled humorlessly. The little girl was peering at me from behind B's legs with her mother's striking green eyes. She dipped her head a little on one side, and greeted me with a high pitched voice.

"Hi!" she squeaked.

I bent down in a crouching position, and extended my hand. "Well hello pretty lady, what's your name?" I asked. She stepped out from behind B's legs, and shook my hand. She looked so much like *her* it was breaking my heart all over again. I was holding onto everything I had in me not to crush her to me, and break down as I did once before.

"I'm Hayley Wivews, I'm fouw yeaws old, and my favowite colow is pink," she said in one single breath.

"It's very nice to meet you Miss Rivers," I answered back immediately, she still hadn't let go of my hand.

"Awe you a police man?" she asked, and I laughed trying to sound light, and care free. Though I don't think I nailed it quite right. She finally gave me my hand back.

"Hayley, that's enough sweetie."

I looked at B, trying to hide the pain still gripping at my chest.

"That's quite alright; yes I am…sort of," I added quietly standing upright, "Looks like your up!" I stated, pointing at the waiting cashier. She made quick work of unloading the cart, and with a swipe of her credit card while the pack boy was loading the bags in her cart, we said good bye. Hayley tugged on my pant leg instead of following her mother, and asked for a ride in the *blue and white* car as she put it. I answered that I would definitely do that, and she ran back to her mother a few feet away telling her what I had just agreed too. B smiled, and waved at me which I returned.

When I got home, my sister's car was already there so I parked my bike beside it.

"Mikaylah I'm home!" I yelled after taking off my shoes, "and I brought your damn Pad Thai," I added with a mumble. This little woman and her damn Thai food! The shits like an obsession. She came bounding out of the den carrying fabric books under one arm, papers under the other, a Starbucks' cup clutched in one hand, a pencil hanging from her mouth, and her Blackberry dangling from her fingertips.

"Busy day?" I asked. She set her coffee down onto the table before she dropped herself, and everything else onto the couch, her five foot three frame taking the whole damn thing. How could she be my sister I had no idea? We looked nothing a like. With my six foot two I could literally lean my elbow on her head or use her as a cup holder.

"You could say that," she huffed, "What about you? Ooh you look like hell. Mmm do I smell Pad Thai?" she asked.

"Don't make me slap you with a bucket of noodles, and would you move your legs off *my* damn couch? One of these days those damn shoes of yours are gonna pierce the leather, and you're going to pay for that," I said. She rolled her eyes at me before moving her legs off the sofa. I set the containers down on the coffee table, and went to grab some plates from the kitchen cabinet. Meanwhile Mika started dishing the plates, and before I was even fully seated, she began stuffing her face.

"Mmm. Thish ish shoo goodk," she moaned with a mouthful.

"Mikaylah Haywood, if you do not close your damn mouth while you eat I will throw your new Jean Paul Gaultier purse into the goddamn fireplace!" I growled. See? Worked every time, she snapped her lips closed, and quickly swallowed her huge bite, almost choking on it.

"Oh, for Christ's sake!" I said getting up to hold her arms above her head, and I rubbed her back as her breathing calmed down, and she stopped coughing. When her breathing slowed, she snatched her arms from my grasp, and glared at me.

"If you even think about touching my JP, I will scalp that pretty little head of yours in your sleep!" she threatened.

Ooh, someone had a bad day.

"Mika? Do you want to talk about it?" I treaded lightly. You never know what this dwarf could be capable of sometimes.

"No. Yes. Hell I don't know," she sighed, falling back into the couch. Yeah, that was helpful.

"What happened?"

"Well, Mark, my boss' executive assistant is getting on my last motherfucking nerves. I swear he's got one more time to call me 'hey you' before I shove my heel so far up his ass that he'll be spitting leather for a month! I mean it's not my fault that we only have nine weeks to plan this Paris trip!"

What...did she just say Paris?

"His ass acts like it's my fault that the owner waited until the last minute! I mean..." she continued before I tried to interrupt her little rant.

"Mika...*Mimi*?" I said more forcefully. "Did you just say that you're going to Paris?" I choked out.

I mean come on!

"Well yeah. I have to go with a few others at the end of July to do scouting for the Winter 2012 line, and to review the designers for New York Fashion Week in September," she explained. I just loved how she answered that like it was the most *obvious* thing in the world.

"Well holy hell. Does mom know about this? Please tell me you are not going to be by your self the whole time, Christ Mika, you're just twenty two, it could be dange..." I stopped has she cut me off, giggled, threw her arms around my neck, and kissed my cheek before stuffing her face with more noodles.

"Oh, please big brother, calm your thirty one year old ass, of course mom knows. She is super jealous by the way, and very happy for me, stop being so overprotective, and suck it up would you. Now enough about my day of hell, I want to hear about yours, did you meet with the new psychologist yet?" she asked, if she only knew.

"You could say that," I added nonchalantly.

"Talk or die. Your choice," she threatened as she waved the plastic Spork in my face.

"Fine," I laughed. "I'll talk," and for the next half hour I described in detail, my session with Doctor I'd-like-to-take-her-on-her-desk, and my little encounter with her at the grocery store. I left out the part where I saw her daughter...not going there now, not with her.

"Belladonna? What the hell kind of name is Belladonna?" she asked.

"I don't know *Mikaylah*. You tell me."

"What the fuck ever. Your name is Collin, and your ass isn't even Scottish!"

"Touché, but at least my name doesn't sound like it belongs to a hundred, and fifty year-old elf," I counter attacked.

"*Must* we do this again?" she said exasperated.

Now let me explain: Miss Mikaylah Haywood *hates* her name, and always gets pissed whenever I call her by her full name, and don't even get me started on what she does when I introduce her as Mikaylah, instead of Mika. Hell, personally, I just love to torture her, and look forward to doing it as often as possible. Now back on track.

"Fine, *Mika*. Can I finish now?" I asked, and smiled at the glare she gave me. I knew that I would pay for that later somehow, but couldn't really bring myself to care at the moment.

"Finish," she answered.

"Thank you," I finished talking about B, as she requested I call her, and finally got to the part were I wanted to throw her ass in the janitors' closet, and do things to her that are illegal in some states…and cue the hesitation. Of course Miss Nosy caught that.

"Ooh, spill dammit!" she demanded with a gleam in her eye that made it clear I was no way in hell getting out of this one.

"Well? Let's just say she's a….she's…fuck!"

"Ooh, this *must* be good. You're all twitter pated, and flustered!" she laughed.

"Okay. I swear to God it's the last time I let your ass watch *Bambi*. Did you honestly just say 'twitter pated'?"

"Yes I did. Now get to it, and stop stalling," she demanded, and I huffed.

"Fine Thumper," I mumbled, "Let's see. I got my first session this afternoon with a goddess, and I acted like a jerk, and the next thing I know is I want to crawl on my knees apologizing, and begging for her forgiveness. She has *got* to be the sexiest thing that I have ever seen walking on two legs, her beautiful emeralds green eyes makes me daydream about 'happily ever after', and shit but even if I didn't act like a total douche I still wouldn't go out with her because dating a co-worker is unethical."

It did not go unnoticed that this was all said in one breath, something I *never* did, I'll leave that to my little pest of a sister…and

him, when he wasn't being a butt head, that turned him almost sweet. Especially when he laughed, his whole face lights up.

Grrr...it was hard to concentrate with all those thoughts in my head. What was I going to do about Brian also? There wasn't much I *could* do. Okay, the restraining order was still effective, but that was just a mere piece of paper. Would he follow me here? A thought passed through my head in a rush, and I panicked. Would he want Hayley? Would he want to see her or take her from me? I just didn't know. He never wanted her in the first place, she was an accident. A happy accident on my part, but Brian couldn't have cared less. He never harmed her, but he never paid any attention to her either, and I know she would have enjoyed time with her father. But now, over my dead body he would.

I pulled myself back to my day, and started sorting through my files. I still had a few officers to meet today, and a few more forms to fill.

After my first two patients left, I got up from my chair, file in hand, and headed to Detective Price's desk. I hoped he was there, I didn't feel like running around in heels, and a pencil skirt all over the precinct to search for him. I really needed his signature to send this to Human Resources. Luckily, he was sitting at his desk typing, not well I might add, on his computer.

"Excuse me Detective Price; I need your signature on these forms please," I asked politely. He was a big muscular kind of guy that I should have been terrified of, but he had such a childish face full of laughter, I just couldn't bring myself to fear him.

"Sure," he said with a wink, and took it as I handed him the form. I could hear murmuring in the cubicle next door, and realized it wasn't anyone I knew from here. The voice was way too high pitched.

Detective Price signed the form after reading it over, and handed it back to me. I turned around to go back to my office, and almost collided with a five foot nothing girl skipping my way with spiky mid-length brown hair, and blue eyes.

"Hi, I'm Mika...Collin's little sister. You're the departments' new psychologist right?" she said in a flash. Wow, if this was Collin's sister, she was definitely adopted.

CHAPTER 6

How the hell did she do that? I couldn't look into those beautiful eyes of hers without losing any brain cells I had left, and ended up accepting her offer.

Because maybe she can help you deal with your problem you have been avoiding for a year better than Dr. Lewis ever could you half-twit! My inner voice of reason told me. You know the little voice that speaks to you in the back of your mind? The one that's always fucking right? Yeah, that one!

Pushing that thought aside I went on with my day, but every now and then I caught my self looking toward her office, hoping to get a glimpse of her. She threw me on my ass this morning when I heard Jeff asking her out. The surge of jealousy that went through my brain baffled me beyond words. Before she turned to look at me I moaned silently noticing her in that skinny skirt, and knee high leather boots.

Leather! Ugh! She was going to be the death of me. The phone rang, pulling me from my daydreaming of inducing fantasies.

"Haywood," I greeted.

"Detective Haywood, you have a visitor. I am terribly sorry I tried to keep her in the waiting area but she just pushed throu…" the front receptionist said in a mild panic.

"There's my dear brother!" I groaned.

"That's alright Lucie, it's my *sister,*" I said between clenched teeth, and hung up, glaring at the little freak who just threw her self on the chair in front of my desk.

"What the fuck are you doing here? And you know you're supposed to register at the receptionists' desk. If my boss catches you without a visitor's pass…" I trailed off with a warning glare.

"Oh, hello little sister, how are you? What a wonderful surprise you decided to visit, and bring me a seven dollar coffee!" she sneered.

"Good afternoon Mika, now…what the fuck are you doing here?" I asked again.

"I came to see you, and bring you coffee…ass!" She put the Starbucks on my desk, and was about to speak when a soft voice floated to me from Riley's desk. I would recognize that melody anywhere, anytime.

"Excuse me Detective Price; I need your signature on these forms please," B said softly to Riley, and he answered affirmatively. Mika, who had probably seen my facial expression change, was listening with a devilish gleam in her eyes.

The lawn gnome that is my sister looked directly at me, and mouthed 'is that her?' to which I answered with a nod, and another warning glare. Then I knew I should not have acknowledge anything because when B walked pass my office the little evil fairy stood up, and skipped…yes skipped…over to her.

"Hi, I'm Mika…Collin's little sister. You're the departments' new psychologist right?" she said in a hurry. B looked a little taken aback, but smiled anyway, and answered politely after shaking Mika's hand

"Yes, you can call me B. How are you?" B said, and they shook hands.

"I'm fine, thank you. So how do you like it here so far?" my sister asked. The whole time I was trying to send my thoughts to my sister as I stared at her, repeating in my head for her to shut the fuck up, and sit down.

"I love it, everyone is…very nice, and welcoming. I do have my work cut out, with the sudden departure of the previous doctor, but you know what they say 'all I a days work'!" she smiled, but I didn't miss the hesitation before the 'very nice' comment, and the look she shot toward me. A surge of guilt washed through me.

She excused herself, and went back to work; Mika sat back down, and smiled a big toothy grin.

"She is absolutely gorgeous Collin. So…are you gonna put the moves on?" she whispered.

"Mika," I sighed "No I am not. We work together, and she is my psychologist. It would be unethical. Now thank you for the coffee, but I have a job to do. I'll see you tonight at the restaurant."

"Did you pick up the present for mom's birthday?" she asked and I nodded, "Don't forget to bring it to the restaurant tonight, see ya!", and she was off.

I huffed…even the road runner had shit on her!

"Happy birthday mom," I kissed her cheek before taking my seat next to her, saying hello to my father, and sister. I had just arrived at the restaurant, and my sister was already making faces at me because I was late.

Ya, ya, I know…some of us have important jobs you little skit! I mentally chastised her.

We were at my mother's favorite restaurant in town. It was chic yet comfortable. The ambiance was relaxing, and we could actually hear our selves speaking over the soft music of the piano. The place was a bit dark, but the candles on the tables were enough to cast an orange glow of light across each other. Every thing was made of wood and glass, the curtains were a light shade of sea weed green, and the floors were a sandy shade of hardwood.

"Thank you sweetie, I'm so glad you're here. Now where's my present?" my mother said clapping her hands a few times, and reaching for the bag in my hand. She and my sister were so much alike, both of them in the same room for more than two hours would cause a seizure on any one who was in close proximity. Plus the resemblance was surprisingly striking. Both small in size, though my mothers' blond hair was slowly turning grey with the passing years. My father on the other hand looked a lot like me, well actually I looked a lot like him; brown hair, tall, lean, and a bit temperamental. Both of my parents had blue eyes though my mothers' were a little more grey than blue.

CHAPTER 7

"So B, what brought you to New York?" Collin's mother asked.

"Change of scenery I guess," I reluctantly answered. I didn't really want to answer, and didn't know how to change the subject before I had to start lying my butt off.

"Some change," his father laughed, "What did your parents say when you told them you were moving from Los Angeles?" he asked. This time I visibly tensed, it wasn't for the same reasons, but still I didn't really want to get into this.

"Mom, how's Sophie's diet coming?" Collin asked. Apparently Claire had this beautiful overweight purebred German shepherd that she's had since she was a puppy, and she loved her like her third child. I'd have a dog too but Hayley makes enough of a mess as it is. Claire began talking about her dog, and I peeked a glance at Collin from the corner of my eye. Why did he do that? When he looked back at me, I mouthed 'thank you'.

"Anytime," he whispered. He smiled at me, and it was like someone turned my internal thermometer to broil.

God, I thought, *am I sweating?*

"Can I take your order?" the waiter said with a heavy Italian accent. He went around the table, and asked for everyone's order when he got to us; I looked at Hayley to see what she wanted and I, unfortunately, recognized that glint in her eyes.

Crap.

"Ooh, mommy please?" Hayley begged. Speak Italian once, and they'll never let that go.

"Hayley…" I warned. I didn't want to seem like a show off or something, I barely new these people.

"Pwetty pwease, mommy!" she added batting her eyes lashes, and putting her hands together begging for me to do it. At least Mika turned her head to the side to laugh unlike the ass known as Collin, loud bastard.

"Don't beg. You look like a dog." I stated.

"What's going on?" Claire asked looking between me, and my *child* as was all the others.

"Fine, what do you want?" I asked. Hayley told me what she wanted, and I ordered.

"Lei avrà la lasagna e avrò la pansotti alla genovese, per favore," **(She will have the lasagna and I will have the pansotti alla genovese, please.)**

I was absolutely floored when I heard my new favorite sound in the world. I was sure I had heard Collin moan. To hide my smile, I sipped from my glass but still felt his eyes on me. Oh that was so not good!

"Lei parla correntemente Italiano?" **(You speak fluent Italian?)** He asked…in fluent god damn Italian! Excuse my language.

"Holy shit," Mika said. This time, some of my drink almost flew out of my nose, and I coughed. Oh my God, this man was going to kill me! How in the….? Why…? What the…?

Son of a batch of cookies!

"Holy shit," I whispered.

"That's what I said!" Mika repeated.

Hayley stuck her hand out to me with a frown, and I coughed up two dollars, paying for Mika since she didn't know about our little agreement. Every time I or someone else curses we owe her one dollar. It was a good thing I didn't use that kind of language often because I would probably be broke by now, my father raised me better than that. I looked at Collin after, right in those darn baby blues of his. They were dark, he was smiling, and I was screwed…plain, and simple.

"When did… Quando ha fatto imparare a parlare si?" **(When did you**

learn to speak it?) I asked. I bit my bottom lip, and I had to close my eyes, and ignore the increased heat taking me over.

"Oh, che è un segreto per una data successiva. Lei?" **(Oh, that's a secret for a later date. You?)** he answered.

There was no fighting it then when he moaned quietly again, and tried to cover it with a cough. When his breathing picked up, and he looked into my eyes I think he got the picture that the coughs cover up might not have worked. Meanwhile his whole family and Hayley were still staring at us with amusement.

I cleared my throat...again. "E come è giusto? Non può dirmi, ma devo dirvi?" **(And how is that fair? You can't tell me but I have to tell you?)** Really where was the fairness in that?

"Well I can't believe it!" Charles said making me jump a little. To be honest, our little private conversation had brought me to a little bubble of heaven.

"Well her name is Belladonna," Mika answered.

"Semplicemente ignorare Mika. Lo faccio," **(Just ignore Mika. I do.)** Collin said instead of answering my question.

"I heard my name you Italian speaking ass," Mika yelled, and I laughed causing Mika to huff, and Hayley to beg for another dollar.

"Farà," **(Will do.)** I answered.

"Grazie," **(Thank you.)** he retorted.

"Prego," **(You're welcome.)** I laughed again. I couldn't believe this; it wasn't rare to meet someone that speaks Italian, but in my short time here, and my lack of social life, I had never met anyone who did.

An hour passed, dinner was all but gone, and the wine bottle was empty. We talked some more, I got to know his family a little better, and vice versa. Actually, I should say that Mika, Collin, Hayley, and I got to know each other while his parents ignored the hell out of everyone. Even having a breadstick launched by Collin bouncing off his father's head did nothing. Wow...It was like they were completely in their own little world.

"Excuse us all. We're going to dance," Charles said. He pulled Claire by the hand, and led her to the small dance floor off the side of the restaurant.

"I really had a great time, thank you for the invite, but I think I should get home. Hayley needs to go to bed soon," I said. Collin looked at my little girl next to him, and smiled. She had her elbow resting on the table, propping her head up, and her eyes kept fluttering.

"Come on, I'll walk you to your car," Collin said as he stood. When I went to grab Hayley, Collin stopped me.

"May I?" he made a motion as if to pick her up and I nodded. I don't know why but I just had the feeling that there was something about my daughter that brought him out of his shell a little more. He picked her up gently, cradling her in his arms so softly, and walked slowly to the front desk. When we got to the cashier, he side stepped me, and *paid*!

"Excuse me; I can pay for my self DETECTIVE HAYWOOD!" I stated between my teeth. He handed the cashier his Master Card, and turned to me rolling his eyes.

"Oh, please don't Detective me! It's the least I can do for being such an ass to you. Just accept this?" he said, voice calm, blue piercing into green.

Damn, I couldn't argue when he looked at me like that, and was acting this sweet. A side of him I didn't get to see all that often, though today he had been showing it a little more.

Yep, my butt was screwed…plain, and simple. Not good.

CHAPTER 8

"Fine, next time it's my turn alright?" she huffed, but then her eyes grew wide, and she seemed to realize what she had just said.

Next time…God I hoped so. No, no, no, this should not happen again! Today was different, it was my sister's fault, and I was going to have a very long conversation with her about keeping her nose out of my fucking business.

I retrieved my card, signed the bill, and walked out behind her with Hayley securely in my arms fast asleep, the whole time I was grinning like the Cheshire cat. B opened the back passenger door, and I slid the little girl in her seat careful to not wake her up. B strapped her in, closed the door, and turned to me.

"Well, thank you for the invitation it was very nice…" there was a brief silence, "Oh, and thanks for dinner, and the help. She doesn't weigh much but when she falls asleep it's like dead weight, and then she feels like a ton of bricks," she laughed nervously.

"It's no problem at all, and you're welcome. Like I said, it's the least I can do after the way I acted, I *am* very sorry about that."

She hesitated for a few seconds, and seemed to be looking for something as she gazed up at me. As if she found what she was looking for she spoke.

"It's alright Collin, I guess I should also apologize for snapping at you the way I did. It wasn't very professional of me."

"No, I deserved it, though I have to admit that you are the first person to ever call me out like that. Brava!" I teased, "So were good?"

She laughed a real laugh not fake or polite. I was damn proud of myself.

"Well alright then...yes were good. Have a good night Collin; I'll see you on Monday?" she grinned, and I grinned back like the Cheshire cat again.

"Of course, we do have an appointment." I followed her around to the driver door, and opened it for her. Before closing it after she settled in I summed up my courage, deciding to just go with it. I took one of the business cards out of my wallet, one with my cell number on it, and handed it to her.

"You know, if you ever need help for something you can give me a call. I owe you one," I offered, and to my surprise she took it, *hesitantly*, but still took it with a sly smile.

"Thank you, I guess I could use your height when I need to get to the top shelve!"

"Ha! You think you're funny huh? I'm sure your boyfriend can reach high enough." I laughed nervously. I knew she said to Jeff she was attached, but I did want to confirm. She looked at me puzzled.

"Hum, no...no boyfriend," she paused, and as if coming to realization she added, "That was just an excuse so Jeffrey wouldn't ask again." She tucked a strand of hair behind her ear, and stared deep into my eyes.

"Oh, well that's good," I whispered, and stared right back at her leaning against the door to her car with my left arm.

We said good night, and I stood there watching her leave, and smiled to my self. She truly was an amazing person. Now to face the family.

Shit.

It was *finally* Saturday; this was perfect because for once I had nothing to do. Mika was busy planning her Paris trip; mom, and dad were god knows where, Riley was at work therefore no manly sports to play, so I was standing in the kitchen putting my morning dishes in the dishwasher when my cell rang. I tensed when I checked the caller ID...B. Rivers.

"You wouldn't," she replied, sounding unsure.

"Try me," I said with a small smirk. I really wouldn't mind carrying her with her denim shorts, and white tank top; I wouldn't mind carrying her up to her room.

Down boy...

B brought me out of my thoughts by hitting me in the chest with her hand, and heading for the living room. I smiled, and went after her. "You know, you're a little hostile," I said.

"Sorry," she shrugged, "I do have a soft side; I just don't use it very much when I get shot."

As we entered the living room Hayley stood up, and looked at her mother nervously.

"Mommy?"

Soft side or not, I could see how much she loved her daughter just by the way she looked at her. She was trying to keep a stern face, but failing miserably.

"You are in so much trouble missy. I told you to put that nail gun down. Now I get to kiss you in public without arguments for a month," she tried to say with authority.

Hayley ran over, and B leaned down as Hayley threw her little arms around her neck, "I'm sowy Mommy."

I leaned against the wall at the front of the living room watching, and my heart squeezed a little. Over a year ago, I wouldn't have cared all that much about this little scene, but now I felt overwhelmed with different emotions I didn't understand.

"Princess, it was an accident," B replied, hugging her tightly, "and it's not your fault I'm such a wimp when it comes to blood." She met my eyes over Hayley's' shoulder, and smiled, "But did you have to call Collin? I'm never going to hear the end of this."

I laughed; she was right about that, and my laughter caused her to flip me off which caused me to laugh even harder.

Hayley gasped, and looked up at me, "She should owe me a dollaw for that."

The look on my face must have tipped her off. I had noticed at the restaurant when she gave money to Hayley, but I didn't question it being so concentrated on hiding my 'Oh-so-obvious-Italian-B-speaking' hard on.

"We have an arrangement; every time I or anyone else curses in front of her, she earns a dollar, and she sometimes takes advantage of it too," she glared at her as she set her back down to the floor and little Blondie just laughed hugging her mother's good leg.

"Oh, well that makes more sense…Hayley, how did you manage to call me any way?" I asked.

"I pwessed the wedial button like mommy showed me in case of emewgency," she ran over to the phone, and showed us where she pressed, "Hewe."

So she did try to call me! I turned to look at her and the expression she was wearing…priceless. Utter embarrassment!

"Alright, so how about you let me look at that tree house?" I said to change the subject, though inside I was doing a little happy dance.

"What? No it's fine, I got it, you don't…" but it was too late; I was already being led to the back yard by Hayley. I could tell it was going to be an interesting day.

CHAPTER 9

Collin decided we were incapable of building a tree house without the help of a man, so he decided to take over. Ass! I took the slip and slide out for Hayley to play on while I tried to help *him* with *my* project. It was a really beautiful end of spring day. The sun was shining pretty strongly by now and there was no breeze, my kind of weather.

"Where do you want me?" I asked Mr. Expert.

The kitchen table would be nice don't you think? I added mentally…Oh, bad B.

"I'm not sure yet where you could stand, and not hurt yourself, let me figure that out, and I'll get back to you," he replied laughing.

"Can I borrow the nail gun?" I asked innocently.

He immediately shook his head, "You know what, I won't go there!"

Hearing Hayley screaming, and laughing in the background made for a nice work atmosphere. He did most of the work on the tree house, and I just informed him that I didn't want to get in the way of a professional.

"Bullshit!" he laughed, "You just want me to do all the work," he whispered close to my ear, making me shiver.

"I started it, and I'm painting it," I replied in mock offense. When he was done I put myself at work, and finished pretty quickly. Meanwhile Hayley pulled him to play with water guns, and balloons. I had a hard time concentrating with my task. I kept steeling glances at him, and to my embarrassment he caught me every single time, but only because he was staring at me. After maybe an hour he came up behind me as I was finishing painting the house, and leaned forward over my shoulder so his face was next to mine. God...I almost fainted again.

"Are you almost finished?" he asked.

"I've been finished for ten minutes already; I was just pretending to work, so you wouldn't ask me to do anything else," I admitted with one of my brightest smiles.

"That's it," he growled, "I'm getting a water gun," he turned, and walked to where most of them were laying in the grass at the back of the yard, and ran off inside.

I turned around, and stared at him with a mischievous smile. "Bring it on, Haywood," I screamed at the same time Hayley brought me her gun.

"Good luck, mommy."

"Thanks princess," I put on my game face, and stepped through the backdoor into the war zone. I kept my back to the walls, creeping through the house, and up the stairs I slipped down the hall that led to the bathroom looking for him. The door was cracked, and I heard the distinct sounds of someone moving around. My smile grew as I got closer. Slowly, I pushed opened the door before stepping in with my finger on the trigger, ready to fire.

"Fweeze," a little voice said...wait a second, Hayley? That little traitor! The next voice also came from behind me.

"Don't move or I'll shoot," said Collin in a no-nonsense tone, "Put your hands where I can see them."

I started to raise my arms, "Take it easy," then I remembered something important...It was just a freaking water gun. I whipped around, and began shooting the both of them. He was too surprised to fire back at first, so I got a few good sprays in. Then my gun ran out of water, and I dropped the empty gun on the floor.

"Looks like you're out of ammo!" he smirked.

"I'll just have to take yours then," I threatened, and he was out of the bathroom before I could blink with Hayley hot on his heels. I raced after them as best as I could with my injured leg, jumping over the obstacles they pushed in my way. We ended up in the kitchen on opposite sides of the white granite island counter, his glorious face flushed from running, and laughing. Hayley was standing in the kitchen door aiming her gun at me, and laughing so hard she was snorting. My earlier fantasy of my kitchen table came rushing back to me making me blush furiously, even more than when I realized he now knew I tried to call him, and hung up before it even rang.

"You know what, I don't think you'll ever be able to catch me, I'll just have to take you down," Collin said. That's when he made a move to shoot me, and I started to make a run for it, but he was ready. He caught me by the waist, and swung me around, and on his shoulder.

"Put me down Haywood," I said, fighting against him. He walked in the living room, and dumped me on the couch, and pounced on me with the little ruggrat, tickling me until I was begging for mercy.

"Okay…okay…I give…up…please…I can't…breathe!" They finally let me go, but as I tried to catch my breath I suddenly realized how close our faces had gotten. Again, sudden images began flooding my mind, and before I did something really stupid like kiss him senseless I sat up, automatically making him back away.

We ended up ordering pizza for dinner, and Hayley was absolutely ecstatic. I think she really liked Collin, she never had a good male figure in her life considering what an asshole Brian was, and he seems to really have taken a liking to her as well.

"Thank you for the help today…though it wasn't really necessary," I rolled my eyes, and he just grinned.

"You're welcome; I'll see you on Monday? Unless you injure your self again I gave instructions to Hayley to call me to the rescue!" he said smugly.

"Oh get the hell out of my house!" I playfully slapped his arm, and of course daughter of mine was right there.

"Ahem…" she extended her little hand.

"Oh…fine!" I gave her *another* dollar; apparently 'Hell' is a curse word in her book.

Knock...knock...knock

I looked up, and saw Collin standing in the door of my office.

"Is it already two o'clock?" I said, and he laughed nodding nervously, "Come in, I'm sorry I didn't see the time go by. I'm busier than a one-legged man in a butt kicking contest," I said with a big grin.

He let out a big laugh, and came in.

"I've never heard *that* before. Good one! How's the leg?" he said, and sat on the sofa after shutting the office door. Surprised of the sudden change of location, I took my note pad, and glasses before settling in my usual chair next to the couch.

"A little soar, but I'll live," I smiled, and settled my self comfortably to start our session.

"Look, our first encounter was not very...pleasant, but I want you to know that you can discuss whatever you want with me, even if it's not of any importance. Captain Broadway is requesting these sessions, but just feel free to talk about whatever you want alright?"

"Thanks. I..." he sighed seeming to struggle with words, and pinched the bridge of his nose between his thumb, and index finger.

"It was hard to talk with Dr. Lewis...and...god I can't believe I'm doing this...I *do* have things I want to talk to *you* about, I just don't know how," he finished. I noticed the emphasis he used about me, and took that as a good sign. Maybe it is a good thing his sister invited me for their dinner on Friday night, and he ended up spending the day with us on Saturday. If he trusted me enough to talk to me, then I could help him better than if we were at each others throats all the time.

"You know what? Let's start this easy, it is my first time working in a precinct, tell me what you do exactly, and from there we'll see where that leads us," I encouraged him.

"That's sound fair enough," he chuckled, his posture became a little more relaxed, and after a few seconds he started talking. I couldn't help noticing the way his lips moved or the way he kept glancing at my exposed legs due to the skirt. My stomach kept doing little somersaults while I tried in vain to concentrate on what he was saying rather than looking at his lips, his eyes, and his square jaw.

It was incredible how my perspective of him had changed. When he was an ass I just lusted after him for his looks, and boy he was not lacking in that department. But now that I was getting to know *him*, he enthralled me even more. He was sweet, gentle, and funny. A week ago I never would have caught my self saying that I actually really liked Collin Haywood, and that was wrong, I knew it.

"Well you already know I'm a Hostage Negotiator. When a hostage situation occurs, we're the ones the officers call to talk with the suspect," he stated.

"How did you end up doing this?" I asked. I was honestly curious.

"I became a cop like everyone else here, and then I got promoted to Detective with the Special Victims Unit. I think it was about a year later one of the Detectives' in the Negotiations Team took his retirement so I applied for the job, and well here I am, though it did require a lot of training."

"What type of training did you go through?" I asked.

"There are actually two types of training style we're taught, the more formal one, structured, rigid, and intellectual is taught by the FBI. The less formal, and structured, more flexible, and street-smart style is taught by the NYPD's Hostage Negotiation Team it self."

"Wow, that's impressive. Sorry, go on," I apologized. He laughed, and ran a hand through his hair then leaned forward with his elbows resting on his knees.

"What do you want to know?" he said, looking directly into my eyes. He had good eye contact, and in my line of work that was always a good sign. I thought about his question for a minute, and asked him to describe what they do or what happens in situations where they have to interfere.

"You know that cops never trust the bad guys, right?" I nodded. "Well, bad guys never trust cops, and that leads to one of the key points in the negotiation. You're making progress when the subject does something to indicate that we in some way are different from the police, when they don't lump us into that category of fear, and mistrust," he rested his back against the couch again, and stared right into my eyes again while he continued.

"We will *almost* never lie to the subject. Quite the contrary actually, we'll try to tell him or her, the brutal, no-holds barred truth. If we lie it's an attempt at a quick fix, something to duck a bad topic, something to shortcut the situation if what was said makes the subject over react."

"We can't lie simply because we can't afford to be caught in a lie. The subject may have certain information we don't have. As luck would have it, I may end up negotiating with this same person on another occasion, and he *will* remember if I either lied or told the truth. So if he asks for certain information I ask him *'Do you want me to tell you the truth, even if it is not what you want to hear?'* Most of the time they're comforted with the thought of us being honest with them."

"Are there any other situations you need to avoid?" I asked, trying to get something out of him that would perhaps trigger a reaction.

"In all of this, there is one word that a negotiator really should avoid. We need to stay away from the word 'hostage'. The subject sometimes doesn't even know those people he has with him are hostages. We certainly don't want to plant that seed in his head, and trigger violent reactions in him or threats toward the people he has with him."

We continued to talk about his job, and before we knew it, time was up. Personally, I think he did well. I did notice certain subjects he avoided or was very uncomfortable with. Especially when I asked him to describe one difficult situation he had to negotiate, his eyes glazed over, and it felt like I lost him for a moment until he came back. For those few seconds he was gone, I had never seen anyone so darn miserable. I went home that night not able to shake out of my mind the memory of misery I saw in his eyes.

CHAPTER 10

Saturday…it was fucking Saturday, why did people decide to take on hostages on a god damn Saturday at six in the fucking morning. I got dressed, jumped in my truck, and headed to pick up Riley. On the way I thought about my session with B last Monday. God, those eyes of hers are just so full of emotions, and understanding that the whole time, I could feel my resolve breaking. The more I spoke with her, the more I wanted to tell her. Our conversation was pretty motherfucking boring. I mean, explaining what I do is pretty mundane to me, but she seemed so interested that I went with it.

The rest of week flew by; I took a chance, and asked her out to lunch on Wednesday, I brought her lunch the next day since she was swamped with work, and I picked up coffee for her yesterday. I was doing back flips since we were getting along so well, but I did have to try to keep things casual at the office, she was my psychologist after all and a co-worker. So we invited Riley along most of the time. B and Riley got along very well… too well. When they decided to team up on my case about something you can bet your ass I was going to hear about it all god damn day.

I pulled up my Chevy behind Captain Broadway' SUV, and Riley, and I hopped out just in time to hear the tail end of the conversation. Perfect.

"Does someone want to tell us why SVU was called in for a hostage situation?" Captain Moore whined. That was exactly what I was thinking.

"Probably because our victim is now your suspect?" Captain Broadway shot back.

"What happened?" I asked a little more arrogantly than I should have. I was irked at being awoken by my beeper just to hear those two fucking babies bickering. I just wanted to hit my bed again.

"The original call was a rape in progress. Apparently our victim, who got the better of the suspect, possesses a gun, and is now holding the suspect hostage. She's claiming that she is going to kill him," Captain Broadway answered, running his hands through what was left of his gray hair.

"So where are we now?" I asked heading for my truck followed by Captain Moore, Ed, and three other officers. Riley spread out the blueprints for Ms. Whaley's apartment over the hood, and we marked all points of entry. We attempted to come up with a plan to end this as safely, quickly, and easily as possible.

Five hours later…still nothing. She refused to listen to reason, and most of the tactical maneuvers we came up with had the potential of resulting in us freaking out the suspect, and winding up with a dead body on our hands. When Ms. Whaley saw one of the officers with us was a woman, she requested to speak with her, and only her. I protested vehemently; she was just a rookie with SVU, and didn't know what to do in a hostage situation. Captain Broadway convinced Ms. Whaley that I should accompany Officer Colt for her protection along with Ms. Whaley's, and the victim's. Reluctantly she agreed, so we strapped up, and geared our selves with microphones and an ear plug so we could communicate with the outside. We approached the house, knocked quietly, and waited for Ms. Whaley to open up.

"I'm here Ms. Whaley, with Detective Haywood," Officer Colt called as we waited on the doorstep. A gut-wrenching male yell came from inside the apartment before the door was quickly opened, and Officer Colt was pulled inside with me following. The door was slammed shut behind us, and a tall blond woman locked it.

We followed her deeper in the living room, and I noticed right away she was holding an antique .38 Smith & Wesson. She walked backward next to the old orange sofa, and pressed the gun against the temple of a man clad only in boxes with a tear streaked face, and shaky hands. The blond who I was assuming was Ms. Whaley was doing her fare share of shaking her self.

"Ms. Whaley..." Officer Colt said very calmly, though I could detect a hint of nervousness in her voice.

"Please put the gun down, and let's talk about this. There is no need to hurt any one here."

"Bullshit! *He* tried to hurt me...to *rape* me!" Ms. Whaley screamed. She was crying uncontrollably. I was afraid she was going to kill the bastard her hands were shaking so much.

"Yes we know that, and he is not going to go unpunished for his actions, but you don't want to be in trouble now do you?" Officer Colt tried to reason with her.

I was against a wall behind the SVU Officer, and decided I should speak up before Colt lost this one, and she decided she was going to kill the fucker. I raised my hands at shoulder height on each side of me, motioning I wasn't going to move, and tried speaking with her.

"Look Ms. Whaley, let me give you a run down of how this could go. Give us the gun, we'll cuff him, and bring him out. Then we'll talk, and you can tell us everything that happened here with peace, and quiet."

"No fucking way, you're gonna cuff me too, and send me to the joint, and there's no way I'm doing that, I'm the victim here," she said in an unsteady voice.

"You are, and that's why we need to know what happened so we can defend you," Colt agreed.

Then the asshole on the floor decided he got his balls back.

"You fucking bitch, just let me go. I didn't do jack shit to you," he screamed. That's when the shit really hit the fan. Ms. Whaley's hand stilled, the gun raised, and a determined expression flitted across her features. Faster than I thought I could move I was across the room. I knocked her side ways effectively making her drop the gun. I threw her down on her stomach, and watched as the gun slid across the floor with the prick's eyes following the trail. Injured, he lunged for it, and once he grabbed it, aimed it at Ms. Whaley and indirectly…me. In my peripheral I could see Colt standing two feet away from the guy, frozen.

I was about to scream at her to wake the fuck up, but luckily for me she seemed to realize how close she was to him, and shook her self lightly. She took two steps, and kicked him in the ribs just as the gun went off causing the bullet to fly out of the window, and hopefully not hurting anyone in the process. I cuffed Ms. Whaley while Colt tried to take a hold of the bastard, and after I was done I tackled him against the wall, and apprehended him securely.

Suddenly the door smashed against the wall, and fell to the floor as Riley, Captain Moore, and more officers filed in. Riley's eyes frantically searched to find us, and when he did he walked to where we were holding the two.

"You guys okay?" he asked.

We both nodded, and Officer Colt went to Ms. Whaley while one of the other officers grabbed her robe lying on a chair nearby. Another began taking pictures of the crime scene. I yanked the bleeding son of a bitch up off of the floor, and exited the house with him in tow. I followed behind Riley as we headed for the ambulance. Once I handcuffed the man to the gurney, and Colt got Ms. Whaley to the second ambulance I got her attention before she left to fill in her report.

"Officer Colt, are you alright?" I asked. Her hands were shaking.

"I…I think so. God, it was scary in there. I'm sorry I froze like that, I wasn't sure what to do," she said with a shaky voice.

"You did very well; I know it can be overwhelming being in this position. You did an excellent job. How long have you been with the NYPD?" I asked.

"Just over three months Detective," she answered. I nodded, understanding now that she probably had never been in a situation of this magnitude before.

"Well, after you fill your report, go home, and relax. I'll talk to your Captain," I clapped her on the shoulder, and told her she did a good job again, and went to talk with Captain Moore for her. She definitely needed a break from this.

Riley and I went back to the precinct after cleaning up our shit. We filed our report and I dropped him off at home. The last thing I remember was entering my bedroom, and my head hitting the pillow.

I was sure I was dreaming, but the noise in my dream was annoying the shit out of me. Finally I cracked one eye open, and it landed on my alarm clock...seven fifteen. Fuck I slept over six hours and...huh I'm still dressed. I heard the ringing again.

What the fuck was that noise?

I realized it wasn't in my dream at all, my cell was ringing, but by the time I got to it, it went silent again. I checked my missed call, and boy I must have knocked the fuck out...I had fourteen missed calls. This time my home phone rang so I hurried to answer it.

"Hel..." I was cut off by a voice I could have recognized among hundreds.

"Collin...Oh my god are you alright? I've been trying to call you since three this afternoon; I called your cell, your house, and even the precinct. I saw what happened this morning on the news, and they said someone was injured, and I ...." B was speaking so fast I had a hard time catching it all. I saw where Hayley got it from when she was in a panic. This time it was my turn to cut her off.

"B relax I'm fine, sorry; I got home around two this afternoon, and fell asleep, but it's nice to know you're thinking about me," I teased.

"Shut up Haywood, I *was* worried you got hurt," she relaxed at my joking, and I was about to ask if I could come over when she spoke first, "Are you busy tonight?"

"Not really why?" I said, trying not to sound too excited.

"Well why don't you get some clothes, and come over? I really don't feel like sleeping out here with Hayley by myself."

I think my heart fluttered, as girly as that sounds. She wanted me to come stay the night.

"Out where?" I asked.

"Oh, sorry, Hayley convinced me to sleep in the tree house. This is a pretty quiet neighborhood, but with nuts like I saw on T.V. this morning I'd feel safer with...you here," she said hesitantly.

I chuckled, "I'll be right over," I agreed, and hung up.

I showered, got ready, then grabbed everything I would need for tomorrow, and drove like a madman to her house. She told me she would leave a key hidden out under a plant for me to get in, so I slipped inside, and locked the door behind me. I put my bag on the wooden staircase and the key on the kitchen table. Before I went to see if they were already outside I looked around more carefully at her home. The first time I was here, so much had happened that I never really paid attention to my surroundings. It was beautifully decorated; it made me think of a cottage what with all the wooden furniture, hardwood floors, and the brick wall where the fire place was situated. The atmosphere of the house was very relaxing, everything in tones of browns, blacks, and beige. It didn't look like she minded the clutter of toys all over; though the house was spacious enough it didn't look half as cluttered as it really was.

There was enough light to see in the backyard, thanks to the moon, and neighborhood security lights so I climbed the ladder to the tree house carefully. When I peeked inside, I found B against one wall with Hayley snuggled into her side. I smiled, and eased my self up sitting next to her.

"Collin?" B whispered.

"Yes it's me. Go to sleep, I'll protect you from your crazy neighbors," I teased quietly.

"Ass," she yawned, "But I'm not sleepy yet. Tell me what happened today?"

I smiled, and launched into my story. I knew that sleeping in a tree house wasn't going to be comfortable. I was going to be sore the next day... but it was worth it.

CHAPTER 11

We talked about his morning, and I don't know how talking about hostages turned into talking about me but it did. Usually I would shy away from conversations about me, but I don't know what it was about Collin that made me want to confide in him so much. After I was sure Hayley was sound asleep, we decided to go back down, and get a drink. When we came back I was about to sit at the patio table, but he pulled me in the yard, and asked me to sit with him. He leaned against the tree house, and I sat next to him doing the same.

"Tell me, where did you learn to speak Italian?" I asked him after a moment of silence.

"I went through a student exchange program in high school that sent me to Italy for a year. I picked up the language, and never really lost it. What about you?"

I laughed at how lame my explanation was compared to his, at least his reason was exciting, and interesting, "Nothing as spectacular as you actually, just for extra credit in high school, and college."

He chuckled along with me, and all of a sudden took on a serious tone, "So tell me, is there a special meaning to Belladonna or did your parents just liked the name?" he asked hesitantly.

I couldn't help but laugh, this explanation was just so much more ridiculous than the previous one. He stared at me like I'd grown a second head, and raised an eyebrow.

"*DON'T* laugh!" I said, pointing a fierce finger in his face, "I was raised by my dad in L.A. since I have been one year old. I never really knew who my mother was until recently because; well my dad never really knew he had a daughter until I got dumped on his door step," I stopped when I heard Collin gasp, and he started apologizing. I shushed him saying that it was really okay, I didn't mind at all.

"Anyway, my dad had a one night stand at a party, and ended up getting my mother pregnant without knowing. She kept me until I was one year old, so obviously she had given me a name. After admitting she would rather party and live the single life than take care of a child she handed me over to my dad."

"So I take it you have met her?" he asked.

"Yes, three years ago. She found me, boy what a surprise. You know those movies in the 70's with all the hippies, and pot heads?" I said and he nodded, "Yeah, well that's her spitting image. She could fit in with the *70's Show* gang easily."

Collin pressed his lips in a tight line, trying his best to keep from laughing, but failing miscrably.

"When I asked her why she chose that name for me, I was pleasantly surprised in a way, because she was very honest with me. On the other hand, I was almost appalled, you have no idea the look I get when I introduce my self. Anyway, she gave me two reasons for my name, the first being that Bella Donna, written separately means 'Beautiful Woman' in Italian, which I'm sure you know," I said, and he nodded again smiling, "And the second reason is, and this is the part where you are *not* supposed to laugh... the second reason is that she named me after the Atropa belladonna."

"And pardon my language, but what the fuck is that?" he asked. I laughed at his expression, and explained.

"It's a plant, mostly known as deadly nightshade; it was used as an anesthetic for surgery in the early days but some, like my mother, used it as a recreational drug because of the vivid hallucinations, and delirium that it produces. So...there you go!"

Again, he pursed his lips to hold his laughter, and replied, "So she named you after a poisonous plant?" he said, and suddenly he turned his gaze on my face, "Though I would prefer to think of you as a Beautiful

he always does when he's drunk, but this time I was not having it. I pushed his hands away, and realized to late my mistake.

"What the fuck is your problem? Come on babe I want you." Hearing his voice, I realized how drunk he really was.

"No Brian let me up. We'll talk about this tomorrow," I just wanted him off of me, so I tried to get up, and when he wouldn't let me I bit his arm. I saw his arm draw back, and then snap forward in slow motion. I heard the sickening crunch my nose made as his fist made contact. I screamed in pain as low as I could. I didn't want to wake up Hayley. As he let go of my wrists, my hands went automatically to my face. Brian reached down, and pulled my shorts off of me, and then ripped off my panties.

I tried to get up but he pinned me down with one hand clenched around my neck, and spread my legs with the other. My protests were muffled by the blood pouring down the back of my throat from my nose, and his hand holding me down. His other hand went for my wrists again, and pinned my arms above my head.

Brian pushed himself inside of me roughly, it hurt, and struggling just made it worst. He bent his head, and bit my nipple until I felt his teeth sink into my skin. I was choking on the blood that was trickling down my throat, but he didn't care, and kept fucking me, thrusting into me harder and harder until finally he came, and collapsed on top of me.

He pulled himself up after a few minutes of gathering his breath, and left the room in complete silence brushing passed Hayley...wait, Hayley? NO. I was used to his ways by now, this was not the first time he forced himself on me, but not in front of MY daughter. That fucker... I pulled what was left of my clothes back on, and rushed to her taking her in my arms, and soothing her crying, she was just three years old for Christ sake, and she shouldn't have seen this.

"Mommy, you have a booboo? Daddy not nice," she was patting my hair soothingly, and that small gesture just made me cry harder.

"Mommy's fine princess." I went to the bathroom to see the damage, and gasped. I sat Hayley on the closed toilet, and looked in the mirror again. My eyes were already turning black and blue, my face was all bloody, and I had hand shaped bruises on my arms, and neck.

I touched my nose gently, and almost screamed out. It hurt like a bitch.

It must have been broken, it was still dripping blood, and I didn't know if it would stop on its own. All I could think about at that moment was...enough, I've had enough.

I hadn't realized I was crying until tears were streaming down my face at a rapid pace. Collin reached out to wipe them away with his thumb, and put his arm around my shoulder pulling me closer so that I was safely nestled in his side. His scent hit me again like the first time. I was getting familiar with his soapy, minty and just *him* smell, it helped being surrounded by it.

"The next day when he left for work I grabbed Hayley, and ran out as fast as my legs would carry us. Of course our justice system is flawed, and all the cops gave me was a restraining order until the hearing. I felt in danger for my child's, and my own life, what was I suppose to do with a piece of paper...throw it at him!" I was getting angrier by the second as I retold everything, and it felt damn good to say it out loud.

"I spoke to my lawyer, and four long months later I was divorced. I am very proud to say that I squeezed every single penny out of that asshole. He resigned all rights to Hayley, that's why she has my last name, and he was sentence to six months in jail for domestic violence. His family had money, and lots of it. I suspect the judge was paid for, because six months was not enough, he deserved so much more." I wiped a few tears away, and felt Collin start rubbing soothing circles on my shoulder with his thumb.

"Hayley doesn't remember anything, the good thing about being so young...she can repress unpleasant memories, but I'm terrified she'll remember one day," I sobbed.

"She's a strong little girl, just like you. I'm so sorry B..." he soothed.

"What are you sorry for Collin? You didn't do anything; *I* should apologize for dumping this on you," I apologized, still crying.

"I'm sorry because I treated you like dirt, and you've been through enough without me acting like a complete jackass and..."

"Don't...yes you acted like a royal pain in my butt...at first...but I thought we settled that! It's okay, I forgave you, and now I don't want to here it anymore. You're here now and...thank you," I leaned my head on his shoulder, and he squeezed me lightly effectively pulling me closer to him.

He looked at me in disbelief, "And for what are you thanking me exactly?"

"Because you took care of me when I was hurt, because you listened to me and…because I trust you," I answered as honestly as I could.

"Mommy?" I heard my girl's little voice from the tree house. Collin looked up, and taking his arm back from my shoulders stood up pulling me with him.

"Hi princess."

"Collin? Whewe's mommy?"

"I'm right here sweetheart, were coming."

We climbed back into the crawl space of the tree house, and I settled next to Hayley. She leaned her head on my shoulder, and went right back to sleep. As I looked up, I noticed Collin gazing at me from the entrance of the cabin like he didn't know what to do.

"What are you doing? Come over here." I padded the spot behind me, earning a grin from him. He settled himself on his side behind me, and I don't know what came over me at that precise moment but I grabbed his arm, and swung it over me.

He froze for about half a second, and pushed himself closer wrapping the arm I was holding around my waist to pull me flush against his chest. Leaning over me he whispered to us quietly.

"Good night princess," he kissed her forehead, "Good night Beautiful Woman," he pressed his lips against my temple a little longer than necessary (Not that I was complaining), and settled back behind me, holding us.

I smiled, "Good night…Jackass."

His quiet laugh filled the night air, and relieved most of the tension from our earlier conversation.

CHAPTER 12

That motherfucking, cheating son of a bitch...
I was lying on a wooden floor (very uncomfortable by the way) awake, and reliving our late night conversation in my head. B was still safely in my arms, and Hayley snoring softly against her chest. I didn't let them go at all during the night...I couldn't, not after what she told me.

Since they were still fast asleep I decided on making a quick trip to the nearest Starbucks. I also needed some space. If I didn't hold myself back I would hunt that fucker down, and make his life a living hell. I could have probably bribed some guard in the L.A. prison where he was, and make him miserable. I got up slowly; careful not to wake them. I went into the house, got dressed, brushed my teeth, and jumped in my truck. I needed caffeine.

Climbing back up the tree house with two coffees, a box of muffins, and an apple juice was quite the challenge. I realized I had help when I saw two hands reach out, and grab the coffees, and muffins.

"Hey Sleeping Beauty," I said looking at her beautiful face. She smiled, and shook her head.

"You better be talking to Hayley," she replied groggily. It looked like she wasn't a morning person.

"Nope...sorry," I replied.

I opened the juice box for a still sleeping Hayley, put a straw in, and took one of the warm muffins waving it in front of Hayley's nose. She hummed, and turned her small body away from her mother.

"Thanks for breakfast by the way," B said.

"You're welcome," I smiled before sitting back, and biting into my own muffin. B lightly rubbed her index finger on Hayley's nose.

"Hayley," she sang quietly.

"Shhh," she whispered, "I'm sleeping."

"Oh, well in that case I guess I'll eat your muffin," I warned playfully, making B laugh.

"Noooooooo," she whined, but she put an adorable smile on her face, and I knew I was forgiven.

"Then you better wake up," I replied grinning. Hayley sighed, and opened her eyes. The three of us had breakfast together. Then we settled Hayley in the living room to watch cartoons while I helped B bring all the pillows, and blankets back inside the house.

"Do you have any plans today?" I asked. I didn't know if she wanted me out of her hair or not.

"Hum…no, not really I was just going to stay in. Did you have something in mind?" she asked back. Good, she wanted me to stay.

"Well I was wondering if you guys would like to go to the zoo. My mother had free passes. She gave me three after meeting you on her birthday, and two to my sister," I said rubbing the back of my neck sheepishly. I've had the tickets for awhile. I had been waiting for the perfect opportunity to invite them.

"And if you want after, we could go to dinner…or something," I kept rubbing my neck with my right hand…nervous habit.

"Are you asking me out, Haywood?" she asked bluntly. *That* took me off guard.

"Of course not Rivers," I said with a smile, "We're just going to go out as friends, and if we end up in bed together afterward, so be it."

The look on her face was fucking priceless, now I was just waiting for the slap or a smartass comment I loved to get out of her.

"I don't put out on the first date," she said, and she never disappoints; she folded her arms, and playfully scowled at me.

Oh, two could play this game Angel.

I huffed impatiently, "I'm taking you on more than one date, genius."

She put a finger to the right corner of her mouth and seemed in thought for a few seconds. Effectively making me sweat with anxiety, would she say no?

"Well I guess I accept your offer then," she said, and I laughed at her antics. It felt nice to laugh like this. It hadn't happened to me in quite some time. She seemed in thought again for a second.

"I just have to find a babysitter I guess."

"I could always ask my mother, I know for a fact she won't mind at all, that's if it's alright with you, and Hayley of course," I said.

"Really? She won't mind? I mean…" she looked shocked.

"Of course she won't mind B. She's an adorable kid, and everyone loves being around her. Now go get ready, I'll tell Hayley about our activity," I cut her off for the hundredth time. I pushed her lightly toward the stairs, and winked at her. She smiled, unexpectedly reached for my face, and kissed my cheek. Her lips burned my skin, in a good way, much the same way when *I* kissed *her* last night.

Luckily the zoo wasn't very crowded. Hayley was riding on my back with her little arms wrapped loosely around my neck. My sister, and B where trying very hard not to laugh at us as Riley and I were trying our hardest to convince Hayley we could talk with the animals.

"Tell him to come hewe," she said, challenging me.

I sighed, and turned to the ape, "Excuse me?"

I heard B snort so I elbowed her gently.

"Would you please come closer so this pretty little girl can get a better look at you?" I paused for a moment, and Riley nodded a few times going along with my story.

"Oh, I see," I looked at Hayley, "She's not coming; I think you hurt her feelings by calling *her* a him."

She looked at her mother with disbelief in her eyes, "Is he lying mommy?"

"How would I know?" she answered with a straight face, "I can't talk to the animals' sweetie."

Hayley turned to my sister, and asked her the same question. Mika was having so much trouble keeping a straight face, her cheeks were flushed.

"Personally I think he's a liar, honey," and she stuck her tongue at me, so much for maturity.

"If you talk to animals, why you nevew done it befowe?" Hayley asked me. She thought she had me there, she should think again, oh small one!

"I don't like to show off," I easily replied with a shrug.

B chimed in, "Now I *know* he's lying."

I bumped into her with my arm again. "Traitor," I whispered.

"Aaaatchouuuu…sorry I'm allergic to bullshit," Riley said, and I laughed out loud not able to keep my light mood in check, and B seemed to be as relaxed as I was. Of course, Riley had to give a dollar to Hayley who was damn proud she caught him cursing again. She was making quite the fortune with him around.

We continued on to the reptile house where Hayley squeezed my neck to an inch of death. She didn't like the snakes so she hid her face in my shoulder, and told me to tell her when it was over. Mika almost did the same with Riley, and he was beaming at the fact that my sister was clinging to him. Well, it looked like something was going on there…*interesting*.

One of my favorite parts was the bat exhibit. I held Hayley's hand since it was rather dark, and the ceiling was too low for her to stay on my shoulders in the man-made cave. I was really hoping she wasn't too scared. I noticed she was a pretty shy child when it came to expressing her fears or sadness. While thinking about this I felt a soft hand grab mine. I looked over to see B biting her lip.

"I hate the dark…tell anyone, and I'll kill you," she whispered. Smiling, I pulled my hand free so I could wrap my arm around her shoulders, and pulled her into my side. She wrapped her arm around my waist grabbing on to my shirt. I wasn't going to tease her over this new found weakness; I was simply going to make sure we visited a lot of dark places from now on.

Around lunch time, we ordered a few burgers, hotdogs, and fries, and settled in the picnic area. It was near the petting zoo, so when we finished eating, B let Hayley go over to see the animals while watching from the fence. Of course, Riley, and Mika, like the big kids they were, joined

Hayley. It was hilarious watching that giant man running around like a three year old.

"Mommy…mommy can I have a baby donkey? Pwetty pwease…" Hayley said with puppy eyes, and without a second's hesitation Riley jumped up, and down clapping his hands together.

"Oh, please mommy can she have it?" he whined.

B groaned, and told Hayley she couldn't have it, it was going to get too big. Hayley pouted but when a goat nudged her for a carrot, all was forgotten. Then B turned to Riley with a glare.

"If you go on like this you are going to be in *so* much trouble mister. MIKA? Please rein him in would you or I'll end up with a farm in my back yard!" B exclaimed to my sister.

"You may not go home with a donkey, but how would you feel about a goat?" I asked.

"Shut up Haywood!" she said, and playfully slapped my arm. I laughed out loud, and put my arms around her from behind. I was waiting for the awkward moment or a much harder slap…maybe even a punch, but to my delighted surprise she leaned on my chest, and put her head on my shoulder. She was brave, confident, and a wonderful mother. Fuck ethics. I wanted this woman, and if by any miracle she wanted me too, than we could manage this 'no dating co-workers thing'.

CHAPTER 13

I was going on a date with Collin Haywood…
After we left the Zoo, and said goodbye to everyone who was now Uncle Riley, and Aunt Mimi we made our way to my car, and explained to Hayley where she was going. Surprisingly, she was all up for going to Collin's parents; he won her over when he told her they had a dog. I had already packed an overnight bag, and we dropped her off on our way back. I assured them I would pick her up before lunch the next day as soon as I woke up. Of course, they told me there was no hurry, and to enjoy a little *me* time like Claire said. I really liked that woman, she was sweet, and motherly like any mother should be, and it was a huge relief to see that since I was leaving my baby girl with her for the first time.

I parked next to his truck, and started to ask him when or where I should meet him but he spoke first.

"Dress comfortably okay?" he said.

"What do you mean comfortably? Where are we going?" I asked, puzzled.

"You'll see. I'm pretty sure you've never had a date quite like this. I'll pick you up at seven," he smiled a brilliant toothy smile, and I swear if I wasn't holding on to the railing of the front porch I would have collapsed.

"I left you a package on the kitchen table before we left for the zoo by the way," he stepped in his truck before I could say anything else, and pulled the door closed before speeding off, leaving me standing agape on the porch of my house. I turned around, and made my way inside, still smiling to my self. It felt like that's all I had been doing these past few days, and it felt great. He really was far from the Collin I met not too long ago.

I hopped in the shower, shaved, scrubbed, and buffed myself from head to toe. I went through my closet looking for something comfortable yet eye catching. I opted for a black, silk corset style camisole with navy-blue piping, blue wash skinny jeans, knee high flat leather boots, and to complete the look I threw on my silver hoop earrings. When I was all done, I did my hair in a low, side ponytail, and swept my bangs to the side to sweep over, and across my left eye. I threw some mascara on, and I was set to go.

When I got in the kitchen to grab a drink, I noticed the package on the table. Collin said something about a package in the kitchen, and I had completely forgotten about it. How the hell he did this without my noticing I had no idea.

Maybe because whenever he's around I forget to pay attention like a love sick teenager. I thought to my self, and huffed exasperated with my lack of self control when I was around him.

When I opened the box, my jaw dropped. Inside laid a beautiful black leather jacket with Ducati written in white across the back, and both arms. I pulled it completely out of the box, and tried it on. It fit like a glove, and I squealed like Hayley on Christmas.

That was why he disappeared before we decided to go to the zoo. Okay, now that was scary. How did he know my size?

Just then I heard a loud rumble outside, and suddenly stop quite close to the house. I was stunned into silence looking at my self in the hallway mirror as the knock at my door pulled me out of my reverie.

When I opened the door I completely froze in my tracks. There in front of me, leaning against the post of the porch with his arms folded across his chest was Collin. *OH. MY. GOD…*I was rendered speechless. I raked him over from head to toe over, and over again, trying to commit the image to memory. After a few more seconds, he stood straighter, uncrossed his arms, and slowly made his way in front of me. I got a *good* look at him then, and oh my darn, was I in trouble.

He was wearing blue jeans, a black fitted shirt, and the exact male match to the leather jacket I was wearing. He stopped about 6 inches away from me. Far enough away to where he wasn't touching me, but close enough to where I could feel the heat radiating off of him, his freshly showered scent hitting my lungs full force and it was driving me insane!

"B…" he whispered as his breath grazed across my face, and I had to bite the inside of my cheek to hold back the moan that ached to escape. When I didn't look up at him, he placed his finger under my chin to lift my head up, and the jolt that shot through me went to all the right places. All the places I wanted him to touch me most. When I finally gazed into his face, I couldn't help the smile spreading across mine.

"B, you look perfect. No one should look so tempting, it's not fair," he whispered.

"I could say the same about you, Mr. Haywood," I replied. I hadn't intended to make my voice so husky, but unfortunately that's how it came out. His eyes darkened.

"Really?" he asked is voice huskier than mine. Uh oh! Not good. Change-subject-now!

"You ok? It looked like I lost you there for a second," he said.

"Oh? Sorry."

We stood there for a moment before I realized what I wanted to say to him.

"Thanks for the jacket. I love it! I would say that you didn't have to get it for me but I know you'd just say that you know you didn't have to but that you wanted to, and then you'd tell me to just enjoy it. So to avoid the entire conversation, I'm just going to say that I love it, and thank you," I stuttered.

He laughed at my ramblings, and asked if I was ready for the date to begin. After I asked where we were going, but learned he wasn't spilling any details, I confirmed I was all set. He came inside grabbing a few bags from the porch floor, and went to place them in the kitchen. Still standing next to the front door I asked him what the hell he was doing but he didn't answer, just swept me up in his arms, and carried me bridal style.

"Collin, what the hell?" I tried to get free, but the man's arms were just too damn strong.

"I'm sweeping you off your feet," he grinned cheekily.

"When you put me down, I'm gonna knock you off yours," I replied with a mock glare. Believe me, I wasn't complaining one bit! He tightened his hold on me, and leaned in closely to my ear, and whispered.

"That doesn't give me much incentive to put you down, now does it?"

I just huffed, and went with it, but deep inside my stomach was full of butterflies. He walked in the kitchen, set me down when we got there, and led me to sit down in a chair. While he busied himself with the bags and started cooking dinner for us we talked about everything, and anything. It was so easy to converse with him, and that made me like him even more.

The only thing I have to say about the meal he prepared for us was: it was Italian, and it was *good*. It was so delicious I almost missed the fact that he was running his foot over mine under the table. When I looked at him, he just winked, and continued eating. He insisted on doing the dishes alone but I won that battle, and we did them together throwing soapy water at each other.

"Are you ready for the second part?" he asked when we were done. I agreed, and after putting our coats back on he led me outside to a gorgeous black, and midnight blue Ducati ST4. This thing was sexy, sleek, exuded a presence, and confidence. It was just so…Collin, and suddenly it scared the shit out of me. Collin noticed my hesitance, and came over.

"You alright Angel?" he said with concern.

Angel? Mmm I liked that, maybe a little too much.

"Hum, yeah. I was just a little more confident when I was farther away from the bike. Now that it's time to hop on, enter 'Chicken-shit B' stage left."

He chuckled before he answered, "I understand your hesitance. But if it makes you feel any better, I've been riding for over ten years, and so far so good."

"That helps a little, I guess. Just give me a minute?" I asked.

"No problem, I'll start it up," he said as he pulled away from me, and straddled the bike. He put the key in the ignition, and revved the engine a few times. Suddenly my confidence was back, and anticipation kicked in.

"Okay. I'm ready," I shouted. He raised an eyebrow, and looked at me for a few seconds, appraising the change.

"Do I even want to know where the sudden boost of confidence came from?" he asked.

"Nope," I said, popping the 'p'.

"Okay," he chuckled. He grabbed my hand, pulling me closer to him, he took the other black helmet that was located on the back of the bike, and secured it to my head, then put on his own.

How in hell could he be even hotter with a freaking helmet on? You couldn't even see his face, but I guessed the fact that I knew what gloriousness was being hidden under that black face shield was enough to slowly drive me insane…again.

"Come on, little Ms. Confident, climb on back," he said tapping the seat behind him. I straddled the bike, and felt it rumble as he revved the engine again.

"Hold on tight Angel," he shouted.

"No problem there," I said as I tightened my arms around his waist, and leaned my helmet-clad head on his back. He lifted the kickstand, and backed the bike out of the driveway, and into the street. I had my eyes closed for the first few moments until I heard him ask if I was okay. I told him I was good so far. He asked me if my eyes were closed. I lied, and don't ask me how, but he knew.

"B come on, you have to see this. There's nothing like Central Park at night. Please open your eyes," he pleaded.

His voice was so gentle and pleading that I couldn't help but listen. I slowly opened one eye, then the other, and was pleased that I did. He was right…of course. There was nothing like this view at night when all the street lights were lit next to, and in the park. It was amazing, and still amazingly busy. In my year here in New York, I never really had the chance or interest to visit the city. It was kind of freaky feeling like a visitor in your own town, but I digressed. I was so thrilled to be able to partially tour the city this way. We drove around for a while longer just looking at the city at night, and it felt amazing to have my arms around Collin, and my legs around this magnificent machine.

We drove for a good half an hour before he took the bike into a trail that even a Smart car couldn't squeeze through. We rode through most of the neighborhood, before he pulled off to the side. He knew he was pressing his luck right then, but I was going to let my gut feeling rule the moment, and it was just saying…dive in!

CHAPTER 14

"Why are we stopping?" she asked. I hopped off of the bike just as she pulled off her helmet, looking around to find us on a deserted side road. The area was relatively quiet, and the dirt road surrounded by the trees was empty of any kind of traffic or pedestrians.

"I wanted to see if you'd like to try driving," I asked, and her face *was* priceless. Jaw-slacked, eyes bugged, and still more beautiful than anything I'd ever seen.

"Say what now? I don't think so," she quickly shook her head, and the motion sent the scent of her hair sailing toward me. I subtlety took a deep breath.

"Oh, come on. It'll be fun, and I'll be right behind you on the bike; I promise I will not let you crash. Besides, I'll have my hands right next to yours, and I'll do all the shifting. All you'll have to do is the steering until you get used to it," I said, and saw it in her eyes that she was beginning to cave in, so I decided to throw in one of Riley's moves that he constantly uses on my mother.

"Please, B?" Almost….

"But it's illegal, I don't have a motorcycle license," she said. Oh now I knew she was just pulling at straws.

"So," I shrugged, "There's not a cop around here for miles," I said.

"Smartass," she mumbled before rolling her eyes, and sighing in defeat…I think.

"Trust me there aren't any cars around, no one is going to stop us, and

I'll be right there with you. B, I promise I will not let anything happen to you," I assured her.

"Is it hard?"

Almost, if you keep looking at me like that! I thought, but then steered those thoughts away. It wasn't the time to think like that since I was going to sit *behind* her on the bike.

"No but it takes some getting used to," I answered, "You up for it?" I asked again, praying that she'd say yes.

"Not really, but…"

That's all I needed. "Deal," I interrupted, "First things first, slide forward. The right handlebar has the throttle, and the front brake. On the left is the clutch, your right foot controls the back brake, and you use your left foot to shift gears," I explained while showing her with my hands.

"Easy peasy!" she exclaimed.

"Really?" I asked in shock.

"No. I just wanted to make you feel better about your teaching skills."

And she called *me* smartass.

"Ha, ha. Did anyone ever tell you that your wit is just the *best*?" I retorted.

"You sound like your sister."

"Nice to know I sound like a five foot nothing Pixie. Thanks for that," I said with mock offense. She laughed, and I took that as her finally relaxing.

"Okay, so the shifting is kind of like driving a stick. You let off the throttle, engage the clutch, shift, and then throttle up again," I said, "You ready for this?"

"I feel more nervous than a long-tailed cat in a room full of rocking chairs."

"I'll take that as a yes," I laughed, "Now scoot up a bit."

She did, and I slid behind her. I placed my hands on the bars, and my feet on the foot brake, and gearshift. She settled into the arch of my body, and I swear her shiver matched my own, and my ass was definitely not cold.

I needed to concentrate…she definitely did not want to feel my hard-on against her ass!

"Now just put your hands on top of mine, and do the same with your feet. I just want you to feel what's happening. It's kind of a rhythm thing, but once you get the hang of it, you'll never forget."

"Is that how you learned?" she asked.

"I wish," I scoffed, "My friend stood off to the side yelling instructions at me. My first time out, I squeezed the clutch instead of the brake, and ended up crashing into a tree. Not one of my finer moments. Which is why I want to be right here your first time out. You ready?"

"No."

"Just keep your hands light, and just follow my lead," I said patiently. She nodded her head, and I turned the throttle, slowly easing off the clutch. The bike began to move, and I lifted my foot from the ground, B's foot closely followed.

We went slow at first, accelerating gradually then easing off, accelerating again, and finally shifting to another gear before slowing again, and coming to a stop. Then we started all over with me carefully explaining everything I was doing. Little by little, as the process continued, she got the hang of it. The movement of my hands, and feet seemed choreographed, and before long, she could almost anticipate what I was going to do. Even so, I continued to guide her until her movements felt almost second nature. When I just let my hands lightly rest on the bars, and felt hers take over, I knew she was ready. She didn't feel the same, but with some coercion, I had us switch the places of our hands, and feet. Now hers were in control with mine lightly atop of hers. We repeated the process from the beginning over, and over again until she got the hang of it. The bike jerked or she squeezed the hand brake too hard at times, but soon, it once again seemed to come like second nature to her.

Over the next fifteen minutes as she continued to practice driving, my touch became even lighter, until I finally let go entirely. B began to accelerate faster, and more smoothly, and braking came just as naturally. I heard her full laughter again, and I could only imagine that she was finally feeling the power, and freedom the motorcycle offered. I felt it every time I rode.

"You're doing amazing," I said in her ear.

"This is great!" she exclaimed.

"Are you ready to try riding solo?" I asked.

"You're kidding!" she gasped.

"Not at all, I have all the faith in the world, you can do this," I encouraged her.

"Yeah, I think I can," she answered, not shocking me in the slightest. She was the most perseverant person I knew.

"Okay, pull over to the side," I asked her.

She did, and brought the bike to a smooth stop. I hopped off, and after making sure I stepped back far enough I crossed my arms across my chest and watched as she took a deep breath, and pulled away from the side. A moment later, as if she had been riding forever, she was ripping along on her own, turned the bike around in a slow, wide arc, and raced back toward me. She brought the bike to an elegant stop only a step away from me, and unable to stop grinning, she ran her words together with a kinetic energy that I had never seen from her.

"I cannot believe I just did that!" she exclaimed.

"You did great," and she really did, it was like she had been riding her whole life.

"Did you see me turn around? I know I was going too slowly, but I made it."

"I saw that," I said.

"This is amazing! Now I can see why you love this thing so much," she said with a look that told me we were probably going to do this more often.

"I'm glad you enjoyed it."

"Can I try again?" she asked.

"It's all yours Angel," I agreed, and a mega-watt smile graced her face before she pulled away again, and rode back and forth along the road. I could not take my eyes off her. Watching the confidence multiply in her with every start, and stop did something inexplicable to me then, but from past experiences I knew now just to go with the flow. Forget fighting shit.

Her turns were executed with a greater ease, and she even began driving in a circle. By the time she stopped in front of me, and took off her helmet, her face was flushed, her eyes were glowing, and I would bet my life that I had never seen anyone more alive or beautiful in my entire existence.

"I'm done. You can drive now," she answered with her smile still permanently in place.

"Are you sure? Honestly, this has to be the best part of my night so far."

"Why thank you," she laughed, "But my dad taught me a long time ago to quit while I'm ahead," she stated.

"Alright then, scoot back *Biker B*," I teased.

"Oh god, please don't start. I can just hear Riley on Monday," she groaned. I laughed, and straddled the bike once she moved. I revved the engine once again, before pulling off, and finally heading to the Brooklyn Bridge Falls.

A few minutes later, we pulled up to my spot at the falls, and we both hopped off the bike. She carried her helmet under her arm like she's been doing it for years. I just smiled, and followed her over to the edge by the water. We sat on a huge bolder, and stared out over the river as the moonlight danced off the water.

"B, I brought you here because this is kind of a 'get-away-from-it-all' place for me…" I stopped, hesitating. Was I doing this? I didn't know why or what but something in me clicked into place, and I continued, "Something *did* happen last year, and whenever I couldn't handle things I came here to try, and clear my head. I want to tell you, but I don't think I could have said anything in your office. This is just…" I hesitated again searching for my words, "It's just more comfortable for me."

"Collin, I don't want you to tell me anything you don't want to, and I'm not talking as a psychologist right now, I'm talking as your friend," she said, gently running her fingers up, and down my arm. It felt nice, natural.

"I know that, but I *do* want to tell you. It just feels more relaxing, and natural doing it here than at work," I chuckled. She smiled her warmest smile, and I felt myself relax. So I launched into my story…

CHAPTER 15

"I was negotiating with a man who had taken his wife and daughter hostage after learning she had been cheating on him. I'd been there for nearly twenty four hours, I was exhausted, and impatient," I took a deep breath, and continued while looking over the falls.

"I need to talk to that motherfucker! You hear me? You find that bastard now or I'm gonna shoot my cunt of a wife, and the girl!"

"Larry, just relax. We're looking for your wife's boyfriend, and I'm gonna find him, all right?" I was on the phone, standing on the roof of a corner store facing the house he was in with the hostages.

"Which one do I shoot first? Do I shoot the whore or do I shoot the whore's girl? Huh? How do I even know if the girl is really from me, if her whore of a mother can't keep her legs together?"

"No, no Larry, nobody wants to hear gunshots in there. You're scaring us all out here, now look I've been trying to help you all day," I tried to calm him as much as possible, he was on edge, and a suspect on edge is one of the most dangerous of all.

"All right, you want me to help you, you gotta help me. You don't know what it's like, man, what I've been through. You don't know what I'm constantly going through…you don't think I got the balls do you?"

"I know you got the balls, Larry, you've got the gun."

"I feel so tired, man. When the fuck am I gonna sleep?" he asked.

"I know you're tired, Larry. You've been up all night. Come on; let me come down there so we can talk. What do you say?" I tried to convince him.

"We lost the shot," Marc spat back with distaste.

"Fine...where do you want him?" I screamed, meanwhile I was going down the ladder toward the front of Larry's house.

"Side one, opening two," Marc yelled.

"I'll fucking put him there." And as I got closer, that's when I heard to most terrifying words I will ever hear until the day I die. Larry, was praying...

"O my God at the end of this day,
I'm heartily thankful,
For all the graces I've received,
I'm so sorry for all the sins,
I've committed against you,
Please forgive me O God,
And graciously protect me,
At the end of this night,
Blessed Virgin Mary my heavenly mother,
Please take me under your protection..."

I made it to the front windows, and dropped to my knees screaming at the house, "Larry, it's me, Collin..." I screamed as loud as my lungs would let me.

"And St. Joseph..." Larry continued.

"I'm outside your house!"

"Saints of God please pray for me..."

"Just come to the window, and talk to me! Come on!" I continued screaming, and now the tears where not just in my eyes but flowing freely down my face.

"Amen."

"It's me, Collin! Just come on Larry...only God has the power to choose who will die, and it's not today! It doesn't have to end now I know you can hear me! Larry, just come to the window, and talk to me! Come on; pray with me, I'll pray with you. Come on. Come on. Just shoot me...shoot me. Come on, I'm right here, just come to the window. Come on, I know this prayer... St. Joseph, dear God..."

The first gunshot rang through my ears like someone shoved a dynamite stick in them.

"Sarah!" I shouted.

I got up, as fast, and as hard as I could I launched my self against the front door. The lock broke, and two more gunshots were heard. There was a lot of debris behind the door, a sofa, a few chairs, and a dresser. I managed to squeeze through as fast as I could manage. I walked through the house with my 9mm close in hand, and whipped the tears from my eyes to clear my vision, but deep down I knew...

"Sarah? Sarah?" I found Larry's body in the living room next to the mother's, and then I saw them...two small legs sticking out of a door way.

Fuck.

"MEDIC," I screamed in my radio at the top of my lungs.

I ran to her, and dropped to my knees...she was alive. Barely breathing, I picked up her small frame, and held her against me. Her pretty blond curls were bloody, and her beautiful brown eyes were looking right at me...right through me. Her breath was labored, and her small hands grasped at my vest so tight I could have believed she was going to make it.

I couldn't see much, the tears flowing freely from my eyes as her little hands let go of me, and her pretty eyes closed forever. I barely heard Riley coming behind me.

"Everybody stand down, get the EMTs."

CHAPTER 16

I was speechless...I knew something happened to him, but nothing of this magnitude. I could not even start to imagine what he had gone through, what he was still going through having a child die in his arms. A child he tried to save, but couldn't. I was quietly crying, unable to keep it in.

"After that, I was forced to leave work for a month, and see Dr. Lewis every day. It didn't do much, he was a prick, and I was a wreck...not a good combination if you ask me. I went back to work no better than I was in the first place, and just concentrated on my job. But every victim was her, every suspect was him...I couldn't differentiate them anymore. So Captain Broadway sent me home again," he said very quietly. I had to strain to hear his words over the wind, and the noise the falls were making.

He took his hands, and shoved them harshly in his hair pulling on his roots. I stood, and placed my self in front of him between his legs. I grabbed on to his wrists pulling his hands out of his hair before he yanked them all out.

"What are...?" I didn't let him finish, I wrapped my arms around his neck, and hugged him close to me. I couldn't help the tears falling down my cheeks, but that wasn't important at the moment, this man was. He was hurting, and I wanted to be there for him, to help him in anyway possible, not as his psychologist but as something more.

Realizing what I was doing he wrapped his arms around my waist, and nestled his face in my neck.

"And Hayley, she looks so much like..." he hesitated, not wanting to say the name. It was easy to see the pain it caused him.

"Sarah," I finished.

He pulled back for a second, taking his wallet out of his back pocket, and handed me a picture. I gasped in shock, the features were similar but the eye color was different. Still the resemblance was unmistakable.

"Before leaving the house that day, I took a picture from the living room. I know I shouldn't have done that, for many reasons but I...I don't know. I just don't want to forget her. The first time I saw your daughter at the grocery store, I was floored by just how much she looked like her," he pulled back to look into my eyes, keeping his grip on my waist.

"I tried to keep it together, in front of you, Hayley, and my family, but that night when I was alone I broke down all over again."

"Collin...I'm so sorry, what can I do to help? I...I don't know. I've never had to face something like this and..." I said. I was good at my job; I was good at helping people. Which was the reason I dove in this line of work head first, but this was something I had never encountered before.

"Angel, *you* just listening to me is already helping more than you think. I never spoke about this other than when I was being pushed too, and it feels...good actually," he smiled, and I knew he was going to be okay, somewhat. I knew when his smiles were forced, and that one was not.

"Wow, some date huh? God I suck at this," he added shaking his head. I was just glad he was smiling again. Though it wasn't a big 'I'm happy and over it' smile, it was still a smile.

"Yeah, you do!" I said. He looked up at me, disbelief written all over his face, "But you know what? I wouldn't want it any other way," I added, and smiled, hugging him again.

The ride back to my house was quick, and filled with a comfortable silence. I took in a few more sites as Collin took a different route back. Every few miles he'd rev the engine, and drove a little faster, making me squeal, and squeeze him tighter in the process.

He was so doing that on purpose.

We made it back, and Collin parked his Ducati next to my Mercedes, took off his helmet, and I followed his lead by doing the same after getting off the bike. When our eyes met, he greeted me with what must have been the most beautiful smile I had ever deserved. My heart started beating erratically, and my breathing was out of control. It took all I had left in me to break my eyes away from his gaze to shake the Collin-induced cobwebs loose, and gain some form of control over my body before I was even able to breathe again. When I finally gained some kind of control, I held out my hand to give him his spare helmet, and was shocked when he looked at me like I grew an extra head.

"What?" I asked

"What are you doing?"

"What does it look like I'm doing butt head? I'm giving you your helmet back," I said giving him an obvious look. He looked at me for a few seconds before his eyes shone with a devious gleam, and that famous grin of his that I loved so much graced his face.

"First off, butt head? Really? No one has called me like that since elementary school," he laughed, and continued, "And second, I don't think that's going to be possible," he said with his smirk still in place.

"And why is that?" I asked.

"Because I refuse to let anyone else ride around with your helmet."

Ugh? What the hell was he talking about? The confusion must've shown on my face since he answered my silent question.

"Just look at the bottom on the back of the helmet," he said.

I turned the black helmet over in my hands to look at the area he directed me to, and that's when a gasp escaped me as I noticed my name... *'Belladonna'*. I ran my fingers over the lettering a few times, and awed at the sentiment of his gesture. It was nothing fancy, no sparkly jewels or shiny-letters, no embellishment whatsoever. Just my name written in pink letters, and it was the most wonderful thing I have ever felt in my life...well except Hayley's birth, but this was different here people!

Without a word, he reached over, pulled me to him, and placed me in his lap side ways on the bike. He stroked my hair, and kissed my temple. I knew this bike meant the world to him, he told me so himself. The fact that he wanted to include me into that part of his world made my heart swell with knowledge, and acceptance that I was right in falling in love with this man. Screw falling...I was already there. I loved him. I loved Collin Haywood. After what Brian did to Hayley and I, I never thought it was going to be possible for me to trust someone again, even falling in love seemed unrealistic...and I was scared beyond belief.

Why? Why was I so afraid? He was definitely not him, so there was no problem there. I trusted him with my life. But should I? Could this all be happening too fast? Could Collin ever love me? Was I willing to risk another broken heart to find out? With much trepidation, I looked up into his gorgeous blue eyes, and when I saw the concern, and emotions there, I knew my answer.

Yes, I was more than willing! With my decision made, I was determined to show this man just how much I loved him, in any way possible.

I moved my right leg to his left side so that I was straddling him with my back pressed up against the handlebars. I wrapped my arms around his neck, and my hands automatically went for his hair. He groaned in pleasure as I massaged his scalp with my fingers, and instinctively, pulled me closer. Our chests were pressed tightly together as they rose in sync with each other when the tempo of our breathing increased. I pulled his head back so that his beautiful blue eyes were gazing back into my green ones.

"Thank you, Collin, what you did with the helmet means so much to me. I know how much you love this bike, and the fact that you want to include me in it, its unexplainable how that makes me feel," I said honestly.

"The fact that you accepted it is all the thanks I need. I would do anything to make you happy Angel, and if that anything includes me being able to be with you, then it's all the better," he answered.

He looked down in his lap, and took a deep breath before he raised his head to gaze into my eyes again, "B I...I..."

Unfortunately, my need for him was so great at that moment, he was interrupted as I crashed my lips to his, and kissed him with every ounce of passion I had in me. He immediately responded, and opened his mouth to me. Our tongues grazed each other, and we both swallowed each other's moans. I moved closer to him, and pushed my hips up against his, earning one of the sexiest sounds on the face of the planet, Collin's growl.

I couldn't get enough of him as I clenched my arms around his neck, and pulled my self closer if that was even possible, but a thought went through my head out of the blue. (Honestly, I could have gone without it, but it was not in my control.)

Shoot, my neighbors were not going to appreciate this if they saw us. Reluctantly I pulled back, but he wasn't having it. He moved his talented lips, kissing a trail down my jaw onto my neck.

"Co...Collin...I think we should...Ugh..." I couldn't remember for the life of me what the next words of my sentence should have been.

Mr. Talented Lips knew what he was doing to me; he chuckled, and he spoke in a husky voice, his lips moving against my neck.

"We should what?" Then he continued to attack my skin as if I had said nothing.

I grabbed his face, and pulled it back, "As much as I like what you're doing, this is a family neighborhood, and I don't think my neighbors would appreciate us making out in my driveway," I tried explaining as sternly as I could. He chuckled again, and kissed my nose.

"Well as much as I like what we were doing, I guess I'll have to agree with you," he pulled away reluctantly. I stood, and got off the bike with his help. He walked me to the door, and took my hands in both of his.

"So..." he said.

"So..." I replied.

Two college educated adults, and that was all we could come up with? We were rubbing off on each other...Ooooh. Rubbing on Collin, and licking Collin and...

"B, you still with me?" he asked.

Darn he caught me. Don't blush. Don't blush. Ahh...who the hell was I kidding? Come on crimson. I heard him chuckle under his breath which only made me blush harder.

Damn you Collin Haywood!

"You know what? Even though I really want to know what has you blushing more than I have ever seen, I think I'll let it go for now. I'm sure if you tell me, there is no way in hell I would be able to leave you tonight," he said with humor in his voice.

"You don't know how true that is," I mumbled under my breath, but of course he heard that.

He softly chuckled again as he slowly pulled me to him, cupping my face in his hands. He traced my lips with his thumb as he moved his body closer to mine, pressing me up against the door. The heat radiating from his body sent shock waves through mine, and I wanted to wrap my legs around him. I tilted my head up, and licked my lips noticing his eyes darken at the gesture. He leaned his head down to kiss me good night.

CHAPTER 17

W ell, I could honestly say that Saturday night had to have been one of the best nights of my life, even though a part of it was definitely not planned. I didn't have the intention of spilling my guts out to her, we were on a date for Christ sake, but she brings the best out of me, and I poured my heart out. Add on the fact that I was with B; we're talking some phenomenal shit here. She seemed to have enjoyed the date as well, and I have to admit that I was nervous as all hell awaiting her reaction, and in true B fashion, she didn't disappoint.

That kiss.

Oh, those fucking kisses. Originally, when she turned toward me after noticing her name on the helmet, her face was so full of emotions that I was beginning to panic. I tried to come up with ways to make her as happy as she was when she rode alone on the motorcycle. What I didn't expect was for her to start thanking me. Right there in that moment, I was just grateful she wasn't upset or worse: rejecting me, and in that instant my lips ached to touch hers, and I couldn't fight it anymore.

I was trying to tell her how much I really cared for her, but was cut off when she crashed her lips to mine. The moan that ghosted from her lips only spurred me on, and I did whatever I could do to bring her closer to me. I grabbed her neck, her hips, her waist, her hair, any part of her I could to engulf myself in her completely. When she wrapped her hands in my hair, the moan I was trying to suppress escaped me, and in return, I was greeted with a contented sigh from my Angel. Taking a chance, I slid my tongue into her mouth, and the electric jolt that rocked through my body once our tongues met went right down to my motherfucking… yeah, you get the picture!

Our kisses became more urgent once our hips came in contact with each other's. God I wanted her…no; I needed her to know what she did to me with just a touch of her lips, a look from her eyes or even with words coming from her beautiful lips.

The minute she broke away from the kiss to catch a breath, and reason with me, I attached myself to her neck. I did not want to go a second without having my mouth on some part of her body. I left open mouth kisses from her ear to her collarbone, earning another delicious moan. Our breathing turned frantic, and it took all I had not to take her right there on that bike, in the middle of her drive way. As I continued sucking on her neck, she pulled away from me, and made me see reason with a little convincing. This woman was going to fucking kill me.

I walked her to the door, and when I saw the emotions in her eyes staring back at me a lump formed in my throat, and I had to swallow just to find my voice. There were so many feelings coming through her that I didn't know which one was stronger. In all my years, I've never experienced anything like that before, and a miniscule part of me was afraid of what was to come. But most of me, including my soul, knew that I was right where I belonged. That major part of me knew that I couldn't want, and wouldn't want anyone else other than this amazing woman in my arms. Every part of me knew that Belladonna Rivers was my life now. I knew it was wrong, but frankly, I couldn't bring myself to give a shit! She was my world, and I knew that my life would cease to exist without her in it. It may be insane, and true it may seem a little fast, but I was unconditionally, undeniably, and uncontrollably in love with this woman, and I wanted the whole fucking world to know it.

But as we know, work is work, and some people didn't care just how much I loved her, so we will have to keep low. I didn't know how she felt about me, I did know she cared…she did more than anyone I've ever been with, but still care, and love are two very different emotions. I guessed I would just have to wait, and see where this would take us, because I could not, would not live without her, so if all I got from her was this, I'll take it, and *not* fucking complain.

On Sunday I went with her to pick up Hayley at my parents house, and we ended up staying for lunch. B, Mika, and my mother got along so well, and Hayley adored her new *Nana* as she called her. Can you say... fucked! When three grown ass women and a smart ass kid get along this well, it does not look good for the men around. I'll just have to make sure I'm not in the vicinity when they are.

We decided to keep our...relationship or whatever the fuck we had, a secret from Hayley at least for now. B didn't know how she would react, and before telling her anything she wanted to make sure she'd be okay with it. I'll never question her on Hayley, and agreed, though being around her all afternoon, and not being able to touch her was pure hell. I survived though, because there were always our weekly sessions and fuck...how in hell I was going to do this I didn't know. Being locked in her office alone together for an hour, and act like a gentleman was going to test me beyond anything I had ever lived through. She didn't help the situation either, wearing those sexy as fuck reading glasses, and tight ass skirts, I was going crazy. But I managed, to my utter surprise, to keep myself in check during my next session, and for the rest of the week too. I had been working like crazy this week, and had to do overtime almost every night, taking me away from where I really wanted to be, with her and Hayley.

By Thursday though, I couldn't take it anymore.

I knock on her door frame, and she motioned for me to come in, without even lifting her head from the file she was reading. We had been throwing glances at each other all morning, except when her door was closed. So let's just say I missed her like crazy. I sat on the couch after closing the door to her office. I crossed my hands behind my head, and crossed my legs at the ankles leaving them stretched out in front of me. She lifted her head slowly, finally noticing it was me, and gave me that warm smile I loved so much.

"Sorry Doc, but I can't take it anymore. Do you have time for me?" I asked, winking at her.

She slowly slid off her chair, and walked over to me never taking her eyes off of me. When she was standing right in front she hiked her skirt up and straddled me, bringing my eyes level with hers. I placed my hands on the sides of her hips, and rubbed them across the warmth of her skin between the hem of her skirt, and red blouse. I buried my face in her neck, and just took in her smell.

"I miss you...this is fucking hell having to see you every damn day, and not do anything about it," I said, and continued tracing her neck all the way up to her jaw with the tip of my nose.

"I know, I miss you too...Collin what are we going to do about work? If we get caught, if anyone finds out...one or both of us could lose our jobs," she stated. I wouldn't have exchanged what we shared or gave her up for anything, but losing our jobs was a possibility if we got caught.

"Well then how about we not get caught," I said kissing her neck all the way down to her exposed collarbone.

"Be serious," she laughed.

"Sorry but I'm finally able to kiss you whenever I want...almost...and honestly that's the only thing on my mind right about now," I answered.

"Collin," she groaned.

"Okay, okay," I laughed again, "We'll just have to be very careful around everyone, and professional while at work. If we can do that, and you stop tempting me, like wearing those sexy fucking glasses of yours all the damn time, everything should be okay," I said.

"Why do I even try?" she laughed, and looked at me from the top of her glasses. Her green eyes shone devilishly in the dim light of her office.

"Although, sneaking around behind everyone's back does sound interesting," she added, pulling her bottom lip between her teeth making me groan, and she held me further away from her...I smiled. Her eyes narrowed.

"If you still want that job you care so much about, then I would advise you to get your stuff straight or one of these days I'll lock you up in my bathroom until someone reports you missing, and it'll be your sexy butt on the line," she threatened with a raised eyebrow.

Oh fuck yes! Tie my ass up!

"You're testing me," I warned through gritted teeth. She sighed, and rolled her eyes before *finally* kissing me. She began rocking her hips against me, and all I could do to control my self was grip her hips tighter.

A knock at the door startled us making B jumped off my lap brushing her skirt down, checking her hair, and make-up on the wall mirror in a second flat, and sat on the chair next to the sofa. I smirked at her, causing her to glare at me. I repositioned my self on the couch to hide my Oh-so-obvious B arousal before whom ever it was came in.

"Shut up," she warned, "Come in," she said a little louder. Riley popped his head in the door, and without even looking at B he called to me.

"Hey B, sorry to interrupt but Collin we've got a situation on the Upper West Side, let's move," Riley almost yelled, and turned back, heading toward the parking garage.

Fuck I could not catch a break!

"Sorry Angel I got to go," I whispered.

"Please be careful," she whispered back, and kissed my cheek quickly after making sure no one was looking through the door.

"Always am. I'll call you later alright?" I asked. She rolled her eyes, and nodded. I went to get my shit, and ran for the garage. We jumped in the service truck, and sped off to the address given by our dispatch. Shit, a daycare... god no...I couldn't do it...images flooded my mind again. I motioned Riley to go ahead that I was right behind him after I parked behind the Captain's truck, and grabbed my phone. I needed to hear her voice.

"Dr. Rivers," she answered quickly.

"B...B I can't do it...I just can't," I chocked out.

"What is it Collin? Are you alright?" she said in a panic.

"I don't know all the specifics yet, but...B it's a daycare...I..." My voice was shaking, my hands were sweaty, and my stomach was down to my feet.

"Collin, listen to me. It's not him, and it's not her...you're the best in this field, and I have faith in you, babe. You can do this, and if I could I would be right there with you...You. Can. Do. This...I trust you, we all do," she said soothingly, and incredible as it may be, it worked. I sighed, feeling a little better. Just talking with her always soothed me no matter what the situation was.

"Alright…yeah…okay, fuck I have to go…thank you Angel," I said.

"You're welcome…be careful, bye."

"I will, bye." I hung up the phone, and put it away in my pocket. God I wish I could tell her how much I loved her. She was so good, and trusting even after what her asshole ex-husband did to her.

I stepped out of the car, and headed for Riley, and Captain Broadway who were in a very tense conversation. There shoulders were tight with tension, and there faces grim.

"What's going on?" I asked.

"Apparently some guy came by to pick up his daughter, and when the care takers refused him he blew up, and is now holding the little girl inside. He's asking to let him leave the facility with her," Captain Broadway explained.

*I can do this…I can do this….*was the only thing running through my mind at that moment.

"Why did they refuse him?" Riley questioned.

"He's not listed as the father in her file; it says the father is unknown. So under suspicion of kidnapping we cannot let a child leave with other than the people authorized," a woman standing next to the Captain said. She was tall, almost my height, with grey hair, and icy grey eyes. Her face was severe, but considering the circumstances it was understandable.

Captain introduced her quickly as Mrs. Hunter Director of the daycare; she was the one to refuse the nut job to leave with the kid. We asked her what happened after she denied him the child.

"He pulled out a gun, and grabbed her by the arm. He fired in the air, and yelled for us to leave the building. After he grabbed my keys, he locked all the doors behind us. Please you have to do something…" she said, trying to hold her sobs.

"Don't worry Mrs. Hunter, were on top of this. Has someone contacted the parents?" Riley asked.

"We tried to call her mother a few times before he went crazy, and locked us out, but she wasn't answering," she stated. The Captain started asking her questions about the mother. So Riley and I nodded, and took that as our cue to go back to the truck, and gear up with our bulletproof vests, our guns, and ammo; meanwhile they were hooking up the phone line to call the bastard. The technicians were trying to tap into the security system to try, and get a look inside using the security cameras, and our shooters were positioning themselves on the buildings, and houses all around.

I made my way back through the growing crowd with Riley hot on my heels, after we talked with the techs. They informed us everything was set up but they weren't able to get a good view through the security cameras. I asked Captain Broadway the additional information we needed for contact.

"Captain, what are the suspects' name, and the little girls'?" I asked with my game face on and trying to relax my self. Ed looked at me hesitating.

"Come on Captain we don't have all day here," I asked impatiently.

What the hell was his problem?

"The suspect is Brian Jamieson, and the little girl is…Hayley Rivers."

CHAPTER 18

After I hung up with Collin I looked at my agenda and...*Yes*! No more appointments for the day. I was in much needed time with my little girl, so I decided to surprise her by picking her up early, and maybe taking her out for dinner, and a movie. I packed up my things, and left. It would also keep my mind from worrying about Collin. I knew he was always careful on the job but still...you never know.

When I turned the corner onto the street that led to Hayley's daycare I froze. Son of a batch of cookies, what was going on here?

There were cop cars, and ambulances everywhere, and the crowd of people gathered together was thick. I parked on the curb behind a Cadillac, not even bothering with my keys, and purse. I ran, pushing through the curious on lookers. When I made it to the caution ribbon I stopped dead in my tracks, and my stomach plummeted all the way down to my heels as I caught sight of *him*. Collin. He was standing next to Riley, his phone to his ear looking absolutely devastated.

Move B, god dammit...move your fucking feet. I chided myself.

I managed to walk forward under the yellow tape, and toward him. A police officer tried to stop me but I pushed his hands away, and ran for Collin. Seconds before I was in front of him, his eyes met mine, and he hung up the phone. I couldn't say anything...the words were stuck in my throat, but I didn't have to ask because my answer lay in his eyes. He took my shoulders, and crushed me to him...and I screamed, screamed as loud as I could, my heart beating so hard against my chest it felt like it wanted to rip open.

"Shhh…it's alright, she's alright. I'll get her out B; I promise…I'll bring her back to you," he tried to soothe me kissing my temple, rubbing his hands along my spine, my arms, my hair, and face.

My baby girl…my little princess…it was him I just knew it was him…

"Dr. Rivers, we tried to call you for almost an hour now…I'm sorry but I have to ask you a few questions," Captain Broadway said behind me. When I turned to look at him Collin didn't release me, instead her kept one arm securely around my shoulders, and rubbing my arm with the other. I couldn't let him go either, fuck ethics, I grabbed on to him with both hands as if I was going to fall, I felt like if I let go…I *would* fall, and he was my rock holding me up.

"I forgot my cell phone at home this morning." My voice was harsh and quiet, my sobs making it difficult to hear my words, even to myself.

"Do you know a man named Brian Jamieson?" the Captain asked. The anger at this confirmation rose in me over powering my grief, that good for nothing, motherfucking bastard…I knew it. I knew something was bound to happen when the officer called me a month ago to inform me he was granted parole. I knew I should have been more careful. God, it was my entire fault. I did like I always do, I pushed my problems at the back of my mind to make myself forget, and now my daughter, my life, and soul was in danger because of me.

I nodded, "He's my ex-husband…Hayley's father." I heard a few gasps from the daycare staff around us, and Collin stiffened, probably putting two and two together.

"How dangerous is he to her?" Ed asked me.

"I…I don't know really, he never touched her…but he never really took care of her or even acknowledge her presence," I clenched Collin's vest tighter in my grip trying to hold myself together.

"He's on the phone, and wants to speak to the person in charge," a man whom I vaguely recognized from the station came running toward us, and handed the phone to Collin. Captain Broadway intercepted the exchange, and Collin looked at Ed with curiosity, and anger flashing in his eyes.

Ed looked between me and Collin a few times with an apprehensive look on his face, lingering on my hands holding him, and his arm around me. Then he did something we never expected, he handed the phone to *Riley* who was standing to the side with an expression almost as worried as we felt. Riley looked at us with a sympathetic expression, and before walking farther away to talk to that fucking asshole, no better than navel lint prick, he took my hand.

"I'll do everything I can, and more to keep her safe, I promise," he said reassuringly, and left.

"I'm sorry Detective Haywood, but I have to give this one to Detective Price." Ed came closer to us so only we could hear. "I know what has been going on...you two are even more obvious than a pink elephant in a room, and Collin...you're too personally involved to deal with this." The Captain was staring us down like a parent disappointed in his child, but I couldn't have cared less at that moment. He could fire me if he wanted to, as long as my baby was back in my arms, and soon.

Collin started to protest, and I could feel just how absolutely pissed off he was...as was I. Ed lifted a hand, and continued speaking.

"I won't ask you to leave, and if we need anything you'll be the first we ask of. We'll keep you in the loop, but for now I'll ask you to step out, and let us take care of this. We'll talk about this situation..." he said pointing to Collin, and me, "...back at the precinct," he turned around, and went in Riley's direction.

"It's alright Angel, I promise," Collin said again, but I could see the fire burning in his eyes.

"I knew it...I knew he wasn't going to leave us alone," I cried, I was crying so hard it was hurting, and the pressure in my chest still threatening to rip open.

"What do you mean, you knew? I thought he was in jail?" he asked softly, his voice shaking with concern, anger, and sadness.

"The Department of Public Safety in Los Angeles called me a month ago to inform me he was granted parole," I said guiltily. I should have said something to someone, anyone, but deep down I had pushed the idea away so far in my mind I hadn't really expected anything to happen. I really believed he would leave us alone, and start a new life without us.

"B, we need to talk," Riley said, suddenly beside me putting a hand on my shoulder, "He wants you in there," he added.

"NO!" Collin spoke louder than I thought was intended, and a few heads turned our way. Collin spoke a little more quietly this time, "No, she's not going in there," he said a little quieter this time.

"I…" I started to say that I had no choice, but Collin turned to me with pleading eyes.

"Please, don't do this…" he whispered, "I'm sure there are safer ways, and more efficient plans than this," he pleaded, "I promise *we are* going to get Hayley out of there and fast. I'm already going out of my mind with worry that she's in there with him. If you're in there too, I…" he trailed off, not wanting to finish the sentence.

"Collin my daughter, my life is in there, I need to do what he wants if I ever want to see her again. God knows what he's capable of, Collin I understand what you're saying and I promise you I'll be fine," I tried reasoning. Though I would do whatever I had too, whether he liked it or not. I loved him, but as any mother would know, my daughter will always be more important to me than anyone else in this world, and he needed to understand that.

Riley stood at our side listening to our conversation.

"She's right you know. Whatever they want they get, you know that dude," Riley said. Collin nodded, seeming to give up. I had to go, I had to see her, and know from my own eyes that she was okay.

"I know…I know," Collin agreed, "Please come with me for a minute?" he asked, and I told Riley to give me a moment before I followed him between an ambulance, and big NYPD van.

He stood there silent for a few more seconds before pulling me to him. I wrapped my arms around him, and he wrapped his arms around me. He buried one hand in my hair, and the other was flat against the small of my back before bringing our faces closer, and kissing me…hard. I could literally feel everything he felt for me through his kiss, mimicking my exact thoughts, and emotions. I kissed him back just as hard, wrapping my fingers in that hair of his, and trying to forget my stupidity over what I was about to do.

"I love you…so much B, I should have told you I loved you this afternoon or even Saturday night instead of waiting until now," he said against my lips. I whimpered, and tried to pull him closer, never expecting the words I had longed to hear for so long to feel so amazing.

"I have been losing my fucking mind trying to keep it to myself and now that I might…Just promise me you'll be careful, if anything happens to you or Hayley, I'm not going to live through it," he stopped, shaking his head. This time, there was no mistaking or misreading anything. He loved me, and all he needed to know was that I felt the same.

"Collin I have to do this, but I'm not going anywhere, I'll be fine because you won't let anything happen to me or Hayley," I said, rubbing my thumbs over his forehead trying to smooth the worried crease of his brow.

"I love you too, Collin, but I didn't say anything because I was afraid you didn't feel the same and this is so foreign to me. I have never had someone love me the way you do," I said, "I love you so much," I whispered again, not fighting my tears, and feeling them trail from my eyes again.

He smiled though it did not reach his eyes, and when his lips met mine, they were hot, slow, and languid and…mine. His hands moved from my hair and down my back before settling on my hips. His thumbs traced paths on my waist on the exposed skin between the bottom of my shirt, and the top of my skirt, much like this afternoon, sending jolts throughout my body.

I pulled away to breathe, and Collin grabbed my hand to pull me back closer, "I'll do whatever I can to get you and Hayley out of there. Angel I promise I will no matter what the Captain said, and he will not keep me from bringing you both back to me," he said with such conviction I had no doubt in my mind he would keep us safe.

"I know you will. It's now or never…" I said, and we walked back to Riley still holding each other, who was patiently waiting on us. When he saw us he directed me to a service truck, and they strapped me up with a small microphone to my right bra strap so they could hear what was going on in there. When I was done he called Brian letting him know I was on my way to the door.

Collin followed me until Riley told him to let me go, he kissed me one last time telling me how much he loved me against my lips, and I told him how much I did too. Then I turned around, and started walking to the main door of the building, I made it a foot from the door when it burst open, and my worst nightmare grabbed my arm pulling me roughly inside, and slamming me against the opposite wall. I hit my head against it, and my back.

My spine felt as if it had shattered with the impact, my head started to throb, and my vision was clouded with tears.

I stood up painfully from the floor, and looked at the man who caused me such misery. He hadn't changed one bit, still handsome with his blond hair, and blue eyes, but the expression on his face was different. Hatred, he was looking at me with so much more disdain then he ever had before. I looked up into his eyes, and felt the emptiness from years ago, crawl back into its place in the pit of my stomach.

"Well hello darling. How have you been?" he asked as he locked the door, and pulled me toward one of the back rooms.

"Where's Hayley you son of a bitch?" I screeched, "You better not have put one single finger on her head or I will kill you," I promised.

"Oh, relax babe she's fine, she's with her daddy." He kept pushing me in front of him to where he wanted me to go, while talking non sense about how I took his daughter away from him, that it was my entire fault he went broke, and was thrown in jail.

I had my lawyer drain every single cent you had, so yeah I'll take credit for that one, I thought.

"Just please bring me to my little girl Brian," I begged.

I tried to hide the tremor in my voice as tears began to form again, and cloud my vision. If anything happened to her there would be no need for me to continue living. She was my lifeline; I loved her more than anything. She was my blood, and I just hoped to God she was safe. We climbed a few stairs, and walked toward the end of the hallway. I brought my hand up to quickly wipe the tears from my eyes that were blurring my sight, instantly realizing it was a huge mistake. I should have kept a closer eye on him because something hard and blunt collided with the back of my head, and I tumbled toward the hardwood hearing a muffled scream in the background…Hayley.

I think I might have passed out for a while, but all I knew was that when I tried to open my eyes my vision was blurred, and my head throbbed from attempting to ignore the piercing pain. The sight before me was enough to make me scream, and want to kill someone. Hayley was gagged, and tied up to one of the little blue chairs in the play room. Her shirt was ripped on the left side, and there were small bruises by her chin as if he grabbed her too hard or slapped her. My fists tightened, and I opened my mouth to speak, but the sound came out muffled. I went to raise my hand to remove the gag, but was stopped by constraints, and a familiar voice sounded to my ears, raw, crude, harsh, and demanding.

"Touch that, and I will kill you right here, right now," Brian said casually. Fighting the pain back with a stick I turned my head, and almost threw up at the sight of him. He had rope, and duct tape in one hand, and a revolver in the other. His eyes raked over my body as he began walking toward me.

"I see by the look in those beautiful green eyes of yours that you are still the little spit fire you used to be. Good, this will certainly be a lot more interesting that I would have imagined. Since there's no need for pleasantries I say we get down to business," he raised the rope he was holding in his hand, and went to grab my foot. I kicked his hand away, and started to sit up but was stopped when the tip of the revolver was firmly pressed against my forehead. Hayley's scream hurt more than the gun did.

"Look bitch. I have no problem with killing you right now, and just leaving with her. If you want to live than I would advise you to cut it the fuck out before your brains get scattered all over this beautiful hardwood floor," he sneered.

"Fuck you," I said against the gag. He raised his gun to strike me with the cross but stopped, and jumped when the phone rang.

Please answer it, please answer it…was all I wanted him to do.

CHAPTER 19

Four hours later...
I couldn't believe this shit. How in the hell did they fucking expect me to concentrate when my girlfriend...no *both* loves of my life were in there with that psycho? Would you have been able to concentrate if you were put in this same situation? Yes. Well whoop tee fucking doo to you.

"Carter. Take the right flank, and if you value your life, you will not take your eyes off of that damn window," Riley said looking like he had the whole situation under total control, gotta love him. I, on the other hand, was trying for the life of me to focus.

"Yes sir!" Carter answered before running off to the side to join the other members up on the roof of the house across the street from the daycare.

The same daycare that *my* Angel, and *my* little girl were in... Fuck! Okay. Concentrate Haywood.

I could just hear B's smart ass remarks about how I let my self get distracted too easily, and if I weren't so fucking worried, I'd probably smile.

But that shit was not going to happen until I got them out of that damn place and back in my arms where the hell they belonged. I hated this fucking guy! I couldn't stand this...what was going on in there?

Sitting here a few yards away from them in a surveillance van wasn't helping things either. Actually, it was pretty fucking ironic if you thought about it. There I was safely tucked away in a steel box with a bullet proof vest across my chest, and two guns strapped on my sides. Meanwhile B, and Hayley were in there with an alleged psychopath with nothing but a damn microphone strapped to her.

Irony…Isn't it fucking awesome?

And to make matters worse, I was forced to sit hear, keep my fucking mouth shut, and listen to the fucker paw my woman. Forced to listen to B's pulse race against the microphone, hear her swear, and hear her beg for him to let them go. I could hear Hayley screaming in the back ground, and crying her little heart out. God I wish they were here with me right now or at least *me* in there with them. My little princess must be so scared, not understanding why he was doing that to them.

The only thing keeping me from busting down that damn door and dropping that fucker to his knees was the fact that B and Hayley were in there. I would never put them in arms way. Whether I liked it or not, which I didn't, she needed to be in there or god knows what he would have done to Hayley.

I couldn't take this shit anymore. If someone didn't do something soon…

I tried to talk her out of it earlier. I was willing to do anything to make her change her mind. To find another way to get Hayley out of there, but one look into those damn green eyes of hers, and I knew I was screwed. It was useless, I couldn't stop her even if I really wanted to. She was a determined person, and nothing was going to keep her from saving her baby.

If I'm not bald, grey or dead after tonight, it'll be a damn miracle. I thought.

When she went in, and that fucker grabbed her, he was lucky Riley was holding on to me. I almost launched my self at the door. We heard everything, we could hear them talking, walking, and I also heard when he *hit* her. I made a mental promise that he was going to pay for that one among other things I was going to make him pay for.

"I see by the look in those beautiful green eyes of yours that you are still the little spit fire you used to be. Good, this will certainly be a lot more interesting than I would have imagined. Since there's no need for pleasantries I say we get down to business."

Everyone went silent when we heard his voice again. We listened intently, and when it seemed a scuffle was breaking loose between them, and Hayley's scream was heard I panicked, and shot right out of the van. I could still hear everything in the small ear piece lodge in my ear. Riley jumped on his phone, and tried calling that piece of shit to distract him.

"Look bitch. I have no problem with killing you right now, and just leaving with her, if you want to live than I would advise you to cut it the fuck out before your brains get scattered all over this beautiful hardwood floor," he continued. When it didn't seem like he was going to pick up we decided to take action.

"MOVE OUT!" Riley yelled. He kicked open the second door of the van, and running after me, the whole time screaming at the shooters to shoot at the first sight of him. All I was trying to do was restart my fucking heart, and ignore the cold, hollow feeling that seemed to take its place.

They're ok They're ok They're ok They're ok… was mostly what I was repeating to my self over, and over until I was able to calm my nerves.

I braced my body on one side of the door, guns in hand, and Riley on the other. I gave the signal, and the front door was kicked down by Marc before we entered the building. I passed through the lobby with Riley, and three more officers. Once it opened we stepped into four different hall ways, and split up. Riley followed Marc after giving a quick nod, and I followed the hall on my right as quietly as I could. I came to five small steps, and once I climbed them I stood off the side to look into the room on my right.

I took my eyes away from the hall for too long, and heard the loud bangs of the gun before it felt like a sledgehammer collided with my chest, and the fucking wind was knocked out of me. I flew off of the five steps where I was standing, and landed against the wall at the bottom, gasping for breath.

I didn't have a chance to check, and see if the bullets pierced the vest or not because the dick named Brian who just shot me was reloading, and making his way down the hall. The bitch-who-better-be-saying-his-fucking-prayers-as-we-speak finally made it to the top step. I looked up into his eyes as he pushed a strand of blond hair out of his face, and he actually smiled as he raised his gun to my head, and started down the stairs.

Oh, I was going to enjoy killing his ass. The thought actually made me smile, causing him to stumble in his steps.

Without a second thought, I raised both guns. As everything seemed to happen in slow motion, I watched my knuckles turn white as my fingers squeezed the triggers. Watched the muscles in my forearms vibrate under the sheer force of the firearms. Watched the bullets release from the barrels, spin in the air, and pierce his flesh in six different places. With a look of shock he dropped to his knees, fell forward down the last two steps, and into a pool of his own blood. I could faintly hear screaming in the background, but I couldn't be sure.

I checked all four areas were the bullets landed in my chest; made sure that none of them pierced my vest. Feeling the butt end of each bullet, and ignoring the pain that shot through me every time I breathed or moved, I pulled myself up against the wall, and steadied my footing before running up the stairs again.

I ran to the very end of the hall where I saw him come out of, rounded to corner, and entered the room. My heart stopped, and kicked back in double time.

CHAPTER 20

Every thing went so fast I didn't even realize Brian was out of the room. We heard the doors being crashed open, and foot steps running. He was in such a rage, he didn't even spare a look toward us, and I was grateful. I kept my eyes on Hayley's the whole time, and prayed for everything to be over. I tried to tell her through the gag not to be afraid, and that we were going to be alright. I was scared out of my mind as we heard the gun shots, and I kept wondering who shot who. Then it all went quiet for a few seconds, and shouting came to us for farther away, also I could hear foot steps in the hallway connected to this room. I turned my head to the door with wide eyes, God I hoped it wasn't Brian, please.

I stared at him, and he stared back for what seemed like hours but in reality must have been a few seconds before he ran to me. Collin bent down to untie my hands, and when he did I motioned to Hayley. I undid my gag, and swallowed heavily. My throat hurt, and my wrists were bleeding from the rope.

With Hayley's arms wrapped tightly around his neck, he just stared at me, and I stared at him. A loud voice came booming over Collin's radio, he yanked the earpiece from his head, and threw it down onto the floor. The metal of his guns thudded loudly against the wood as he dropped them when he unhooked his holster, and landed next to his feet. He whispered to Hayley, and as she realized she was free from the chair she reached out to me with a loud cry. Collin passed her from his arms to mine, and I hugged her with all my strength. I stared up at Collin, and was at a lost for words as my tears flowed freely. Flinching, and biting his lip, he removed his vest, and it fell to the floor with the rest of his gear before he bent down with us. The entire time, his eyes never left mine.

I broke down before he even reached us. Collin's arms were around my waist and Hayley's little frame before I collapsed onto his chest as the tears, seeing their chance, flowed with even more force. It was like his touch was the key to the floodgates, and boy did they open.

"I'm…sorry…it's all…my…fault," I sobbed against his chest, feeling nothing but remorse, and sadness. Hayley never letting go of my neck cried louder, and screamed at Collin's touch.

"It's me princess, you're safe…it's over baby girl," Collin said, and she turned her head launching herself in his arms again. He squeezed her tighter, and pulled me in with them.

I wrapped my arms around his neck.

"Thank you Collin, thank you, thank you, thank you…" I repeated over, and over.

As I cried, I felt his heavy breathing, heard his mutters of prayers, and thanks, and felt his heart beating rapidly against his chest. Swallowing my sobs, but not releasing my grip on him, I raised my head, and almost gasped at what I saw. He looked…I mean I've never seen him so…. my heart was hurting even more.

"I pro…" he started, stopping to clear his throat, and closed his eyes, "I promised I would get you out of here, both of you," he finished in a voice so soft, but still powerful enough to render me breathless. I just sat there gasping, unable to speak, not knowing what to say, but knowing this was my entire fault. I sobbed another apology, and marveled at the catch in his voice when he said that he loved us, and that it was no ones fault but *his,* before pulling us closer against him. His grip on me crushed Brian's in the dust…and I loved it.

I heard the pounding on the floor of the hallway, and the blare coming out of his radio a few feet away from us, at the same time Collin did. The door flew open again, and a raised gun entered the room before the head of a worried Riley followed. His head searched the children's room before his eyes landed on us. I didn't know if he wanted to smile or punch something. Instead, he decided to sigh with relief before pushing the door open all the way, and letting the other officers in. Hearing the footsteps, Collin raised his head, and began removing his arms from me, but kept a firm hold of Hayley. I freaked out, thinking he was about to make me move off of him, and tightened my grip on his neck. Finally, *finally*, I saw the smile that begins my days, and encompasses my nights. He placed his finger under my chin, and looked at my lips before lowering his mouth to mine, and kissing me until they stung. I weaved my hands through his hair, and pulled us closer together careful not to crush Hayley in between us. I could taste my tears as I wept with relief, and happiness, and a whole plethora of mushy stuff. Collin just groaned against my mouth, and deepened the kiss.

Once the lips were removed he pulled us down to the floor, and sat back on his heels to look us over. He lightly fingered the bruise on the side of my face, the bump on the back of my head, and Hayley's bruises on her chin, and arms.

As more of the other officers began to enter, he noticed my torn clothes. So he gently pulled Hayley's arms from his neck, and leaned forward to pull his shirt off over his head, and placing it over mine. I slid my arms through the sleeves, and I saw the four round bullet shaped bruises on his chest, and the blue tint around his ribs, and wanted to cry or kick something all over again. Hayley almost immediately attached herself to us again.

I clenched my hands into tight fists, and tried to steady my staggered breathing. Collin raised his hand, and wiped away a stray tear from my cheek with his warm thumb. He then dropped his head to my shoulder, and released a deep shuddering breath while wrapping his arms completely around us both, and pulled us against his body as close as possible.

I *kissed* his hair…I *breathed* in his scent…I *felt* his breathing…I *listened* to the thrum of his heart, making myself believe that we were actually here, he was holding us, and breathing in the same air. That was all I gave a damn about at that moment. That was all I'd ever give a damn about from that point on…we were alive.

I couldn't even tell how long we stayed on the floor like this but after a while he gathered us, and we exited the building. A bunch of officers came to us, bringing a blanket for me, and Hayley.

"Miss, we need you to come with us for examination," an EMT told me. He looked very young, but very sweet. So I decided to stay polite instead of telling him to 'stick it where the sun don't shine'.

"I'm fine, but Hay…"

"Sweetheart, we need to get you, and Hayley checked out, it's standard procedure. You have to go to the hospital," Collin said with worry lacing his voice.

I nodded, I didn't feel like arguing, and I really wanted my little girl to get medical attention. So I reluctantly stepped inside the ambulance, Collin handed Hayley over to me but to my surprise she didn't want to let him go.

"Princess, you have to go see a doctor. We need to make sure you're not hurt alright?" he told her, while rubbing her back, and kissing her forehead.

For the first time in hours she spoke, and her voice was rough, and scratchy from crying, "I…pwease stay," she whispered holding on to him tighter, and my heart squeezed. She loved him so much; it was apparent in her eyes just how much she truly did.

"I'll be right there, sweetie. I can't go in the ambulance with you, but I'll see you at the hospital," he said with such conviction she loosened her grip, and came to me.

"Pwomise?" she asked.

"I promise, and I keep my promises," he kissed her forehead again, and leaned in to softly kiss my lips, holding my face with both hands.

"Ti amo, B…così tanto," **(I love you B…so much)** my eyes stung with tears again, and I kissed him back with all I had.

"Ti amo troppo e non si è sbarazzarsi di me," **(I love you too, and you're not getting rid of me)** I replied. He laughed quietly, and stoked my bottom lip with his thumb.

"Spero di no." **(I hope not)** He slowly stepped out, and after another quick goodbye an EMT climbed in with us, and closed the door. We felt the ambulance move forward on our way to the hospital.

It felt like days since we last saw Collin. We've been here for two hours, and he still hadn't made it in yet. I was in a private room waiting for my Hayley to come back. A nurse took her for a few tests to make sure she had no internal bleeding, and other injuries. They wouldn't let me go with her even when I protested. They were saying something about me having a concussion, and I needed to stay in bed. They even wanted to keep me overnight…over my dead body they would. I hated hospitals.

"Excuse me?" I asked a nurse passing in front of my room, "Do you know how much longer until my daughter comes back from her tests… please?" I was impatient but I could still be polite, it wasn't really her fault I was stuck in this god forsaken bed.

"I'm sorry I don't, let me check with the front desk, what's her name?" she asked in a very annoying nasal voice. She was small, and a bit on the chubby side. Her hair was messy, in a tight bun on the top of her head.

"Thank you, Hayley Rivers," and now the waiting game again, it took her almost thirty minutes to get back to me with an answer.

"Miss? She's on her way back up."

Good, now where the hell is Collin. I thought. I wanted to see him; I *needed* to have him next to me. Hayley came back a few minutes later one hand holding the nurse's, and the other holding a lollipop.

"Look mommy, the lady gave me candy!" she yelled.

"That's great, honey. Come here, mommy missed you," she climbed in bed with my help, and nestled against me. She was such a brave little squirt.

"There are my girls!"

If I could have I would have jumped out of bed and into his arms when I saw his head pop out of the door frame, but the girl in my arms wouldn't let me do that. She beat me to it. As soon as Collin was about two feet from the bed she stood, and jumped in his arms. He caught her with ease, and hugged her tightly against his chest, closing his eyes, and whispering to her.

"How's my little princess? I missed you so much, I'm sorry to be so late I had to stay a little longer," he said.

"It's okay," her little voice quivered. Collin came next to my bed, and I scooted over as much as I could to leave room for him to sit next to me. He settled in with his back against the plastic pillow, putting Hayley on his chest and me under his arm, and kissed my forehead lovingly.

"I am sorry for being late; Ed wanted to talk to me. I tried to get out of there as fast as I could," he said guiltily.

"It's alright…I just…I really wanted you here, but you're here now that's all that matters." I scooted closer, as close as could. If I could have crawled under his skin I would have. "What did Broadway want?" I asked.

"It's not important; we can talk about it later. You and Hayley need to rest."

We looked over at her, and she was sound asleep with her lollipop sticking out of her mouth. Collin chuckled, and pulled it out carefully, throwing it in the garbage can next to the bed.

"How are you?" he asked, worry shining in his eyes.

"Fine, a little headache, but over all I feel okay. They want me to stay over night, something about a concussion, and they're going to give me the results for Hayley's tests in a while…how about you?"

"I'm alright, don't worry about me you guys are what's important right now. Close your eyes Angel, sleep a little, I'm not going anywhere," he said.

I didn't feel like arguing with him about what was important, but I will shove it in his head one day that he is as important to me as my daughter. I would have done the same thing I did today if it would have been his life that was in danger. So, I just reached up, and kissed him slowly, rested my head against his shoulder, and went to sleep, feeling more safe, and happy than I ever felt before.

CHAPTER 21

I watched the ambulance leave with a heavy heart. I longed to be in there with them, to stay as close as I could to them, but rules were rules, and I had things to own up to before I could leave. I went back inside the daycare to retrieve my gear from the floor where I left them, and then walked to my service truck for another shirt. I always kept a bag of clothes in it for emergencies. I was about to climb in, when I heard my name.

"Haywood, get your ass over here right fucking now!" Captain Broadway yelled. Shit. He pointed a finger toward the building and started talking, "What the hell was that? I thought I told you to STAY OUT OF IT."

"With all due respect Captain…but fuck you. How would you have reacted if it would have been your wife in there with your son?" I screamed right back at him.

"She is not your wife Collin, and she is not your child. When your boss tells you to…" he said, but I cut him off right there.

"Bullshit, I love her more than anything in this world, and I love that little girl like she was my own so don't give me that 'it's different' crap because I'm not buying it," I was pissed…beyond pissed, I just wanted to tell him to take his job, and shove it.

"You know as well as I do that if your wife and your son would have been in there, you would have done the same fucking thing," I screamed in his face.

"Meet me at the precinct Collin we need to talk about this," he said abruptly, turned around, and headed for his car, red faced, and stomping.

Well fuck!

He was sitting at his desk waiting for me, hands crossed in front of him, and a stern look on his face.

"Sit," he commanded.

I almost opened my mouth to tell him that I wasn't his fucking dog, but in that circumstance, shutting up would have been the better choice. I sat in the chair opposite his desk, and waited for him to continue.

"So…I guess I'll be expecting your badge, guns, and keys on my desk, as well as both your resignation letters?"

"WHAT?" I yelled. My jaw dropped, so it had come that?

"You know the rules Haywood, no relationship between co-workers are tolerated, even the administrative staff."

"Don't you think Belladonna should be here for this conversation? It's only fair,"…*ass*…I added in my head.

A slow smile crept on his face, and now my ass was fucking confused.

"Look Haywood, I'm sorry. I should have said something to the both of you when I realized what was going on, but I didn't want to risk losing one of the best Detectives, and psychologist that this department has seen in years," he said, smiling. If a bug would have flown into my damn mouth, I wouldn't have been shocked at all.

"Now grant it, your attitude could use a little tweaking," he added, quickly glancing at me. I fought the urge to stick out my tongue; I'm telling you it was hard.

"And yes I wish your disciplinary file wasn't quite so large," he complained, "But I would have had to be blind, and a terrible officer of the law not to see the chemistry, the magnetism between the both of you. I really am sorry but you have to go, both of you. I'll talk with her my self when she feels better."

"Captain, she just started here, this is my fault. I'll go, but don't fire her," I begged. I was not going to let this ruin B's career.

"I'll need a resignation letter for the Negotiations Team, and one for the entire department," he sighed, "As for Doctor Rivers I'll deal with that my self. Collin, if I don't fire the both you, I could risk losing my job over this and Riley's too. He knew about it, and kept silent. But I am not about to loose my entire staff because of you two. Don't worry about Doctor Rivers; I'll make sure she has the best references possible from me."

"Captain, you can't possibly..."

"I'm sorry, Collin, rules are rules," he said. I sighed, and stood up to leave.

"You'll have my letter on your desk soon enough," I threw the keys to the Service truck, my badge, and my guns on his desk, and headed for the door.

"Collin?" he stood up, and looked at me with an amused expression. God this man must be bi-fucking-polar.

"I'll expect your resignation on my desk as soon as possible," he said, smiling at my scowl before quickly finishing, "And I'll wait for Lieutenant Haywood's application on my desk *as soon as possible.*"

"Excuse me?" That stopped me dead in my tracks. What the fuck was he talking about?

"I have a friend that works for the FBI. I'll forward the letters of recommendation, and your commendations along with your file once I receive it," he finished. Finally, he sat in his chair, and looked at me as the silence again reigned supreme in the room.

"Sir, why are you doing this?" I asked. I didn't want to push my luck, but I had to know.

"I told you Collin, you're a good cop, and you don't deserve to be sacked for something this stupid. Though you do deserve it for telling me off..." he glared.

"Yeah, sorry about that," I answered sheepishly rubbing a hand on the back of my neck.

"I understand where you come from, it's alright. Now go, I'm sure you're anxious to see them." He waved me out, and I nodded, thanked him about fifty times, and after he reminded me he needed my resignation letters as quickly as possible I was out of there like a bat out of hell.

When I got to the hospital, the lady at the front desk directed me to B's room, and when I saw my two girls it was like ten ton was lifted off my shoulders. They were here and they were safe.

B slept for a few hours, and when the Doctor came in with Hayley's' results I didn't want to wake them up. The results came in negative for the internal bleeding, and they didn't see anything wrong with her apart from a few bumps and bruises. Another few tones lifted off my shoulders. I pleaded a little with the doctor to let me bring them home instead of staying here, and after a little begging he conceded.

"On one condition Mr. Haywood, you need to keep an eye on Miss Rivers. Her concussion is not severe but if you notice her getting dizzy or disoriented, if she feels nauseous or her headache goes on for too long, you *HAVE* to bring her back as quickly as you can., and you'll need to wake her up every two hours or so to make sure she stays conscious. *Understood?*" he said, making his point very clear. He looked a little like a drill sergeant, you know the type, broad shoulders not very tall but looks like he could kick your ass from here to Japan. So I agreed to his condition, without arguing.

"Of course, thank you Doctor."

"I'll go sign the release papers for both of them, and then you can leave," he said looking at his chart, and walking out of the room. He came back about fifteen minutes later, and after thanking him again I softly tried to wake up B without disturbing Hayley.

"Angel, wake up," I whispered, running my fingers along the perfect lines of her face. I kissed her nose, her eyes, and her cheeks, when I reached the corner of her mouth I felt her smile.

"Rise and shine beautiful...well it's not exactly sunny, but you get the point," I whispered again. I didn't want to wake Hayley. Poor thing was absolutely exhausted and snoring on my chest. B giggled quietly.

"What time is it?" she asked voice groggy, and sleepy.

"It's nearly midnight, and time to go. The doctor came, Hayley's tests results are perfectly fine, and he signed your release papers," I informed her.

"Really? That's great, so we can go home?" she asked, a little more awake now.

"Yes, but on one condition, the doc says I have to keep a close eye on you. So…you're place or mine, sweet thing?" I wiggled my eyebrows attempting to make her laugh. It worked. She burst out loud, and then muffled her laughter with my shoulder trying not to wake up Hayley.

"Wow, that was so cheesy!" she said still giggling when she seemed to realize something. "Wait, I don't have my car, and you don't have a car seat. How are we gonna leave?"

"Took care of it. I left the service truck at the precinct, took a cab, and picked up your car to come over here…it's a good thing you left your keys in the ignition. Though you're lucky it didn't get stolen," I said with a reproaching glance.

"You thought of everyth…Oh shoot, I did? God, thank my lucky stars the daycare is in a good neighborhood," she said with relief.

"Damn right! Now let's get you girls' home," I said making her laugh lightly again, and I couldn't resist kissing her beautiful smiling mouth.

CHAPTER 22

The ride home was silent; Collin settled a sleeping Hayley in her seat, and drove us to my house. He did have to stop home quickly to grab a bag of clothes, and necessities though. My little angel never woke up, even when he picked her up, carried her to her bedroom, and I changed her into some comfortable pajamas. She did squirm a little but poor thing was so exhausted she knocked right out again. I told her good night, that I loved her, and kissed her cheek lovingly. When I turned to exit the room I noticed Collin wasn't following me, he was sitting on the edge of her bed. He leaned down, brushed a curl of hair away from her face, and kissed her forehead.

He whispered to her how much he loved her, that he was going to make sure nothing ever happened to her again, and how much he loved me. *Me.* I still couldn't believe it. My eyes filled with tears, and my heart swelled twice its size, I felt like the Grinch on Christmas.

I hadn't even noticed he got up, and stood in front of me.

"Come on Angel, you're as tired as she is," he whispered, I nodded letting him lead me to my room. I just settled for a quick shower, and buried my self in my blankets until Collin finished his own. I was about to fall asleep when I felt two warm, strong arms wrap me up, and pull me. I turned on my side so I was facing him, and buried my face in his chest, wrapping my own arms around him.

"I lo…" he cleared his throat, and tried again. "Ti amo così tanto, non posso immaginare la mia vita senza di te," **(I love you so much; I can not**

117

imagine my life now, without you.) he spoke softly, but I could hear the tremor in his voice.

"I love you too Collin, non ho idea di cosa farei senza di te." **(I have no idea what I would do without you.)** I smiled, and kissed up his collar bone earning a low moan from him when I reached his neck, and I smiled even wider. Screw my headache, I know the perfect cure.

I groaned as his mouth crashed hungrily onto mine. His hands twisted in my hair gently, and the combined sensations of his tongue in my mouth, and his body now on top of mine made me whimper. His hand drifted down my leg, and he swiftly hitched it around his waist. With a low growl, Collin buried his face in my neck as his pelvis pressed against mine. I moaned softly...but then he pushed against me again...and again....and I couldn't contain the breathy moan that escaped my body.

"God, I love that sound..." Collin said. His breath tickled the skin of my neck as he peppered kisses along my collar bone. I gripped his shoulders firmly, wrapped my legs around his waist, rocking against him as his mouth hungrily swept across mine again, and again.

I moaned when he pulled me tighter against him. His hips gently moved against mine, and I trembled with need. My eyes closed with pleasure as his tongue outlined the shell of my ear. I arched against him, and I could feel his grin against my skin.

"Per favore..." **(Please)** I begged. His lips trailed kisses along the side of my neck.

"Ti darò tutto..." **(I'll give you anything)** he murmured softly as his eyes found mine again. He pressed his forehead against mine, "Ti darò tutto quello che volete..." **(I'll give you anything you want)**

"Voglio solo che tu..." **(I just want you)** I whispered roughly, "Solo tu...." **(Only you)**

"Sei così bella," **(You are so beautiful)** he whispered longingly as he stroked my nose with his, "I don't tell you enough."

"You tell me all the time," I promised him.

With a smile, he reached up, and unbuttoned my shirt one button at a time, kissing my chest all the way down until he was done, and came back up. Our bare chests pressed together were just too much, and with a whimper I brought his mouth to mine. His tongue found its way into my mouth, and I savored the feeling, the taste. Losing my self in the touch, the feel, and the scent of this man who loved me so completely was the easiest thing I ever had to do. I could feel him pressed against me, and through my haze I heard my voice begging him to remove the last barriers that remained between us.

"I need you..." I whispered breathlessly as I clutched at the bedspread.

"I know, Angel...I need you too...." he murmured as he rose above me. I felt his length press against me, and I opened my legs as an invitation. His forehead fell to mine, and his blue eyes never faltered as he slowly.... so slowly....entered me. Our mutual sighs and moans of pleasure were replaced with soft, sweet kisses as he pulled away, and pushed into me once again...gently and carefully...as if he was testing us, testing our control, testing our bodies. There was no awkward positioning or hesitant movements. If there had ever been uncertainty, each slow thrust as he entered my body cast all of those doubts away.

God himself did make us into corresponding shapes, like puzzle pieces from the clay. I was made for him...he was made for me, and with that revelation; I lifted my hips allowing him to fill me completely.

Collin groaned as his body covered mine, and our kisses became hungrier as his thrusts quickly became frantic. He buried his face in my hair, and whispered my name. Hearing my name on his lips caused my muscles to clench around him, and he growled with pleasure. Without breaking our connection he quickly sat on his heels, lifting me onto his lap, and I encircled his waist with my legs shrugging off my unbuttoned shirt.

I arched my body back as he grabbed my hips, and thrust harder. His other hand drifted to my breast, and I moaned as his fingertips ghosted along my skin. The sensation was electric but nothing could have prepared me for the moment Collin took me into his mouth. I whimpered loudly as he drove deeper, and I felt it....that long dormant sensation that made my stomach clench with want, and desire.

"I love you," he growled huskily as he pulled my body against his once again. That was all he said, but it was enough...and within seconds....I was moaning as my body convulsed around him. I breathlessly replied my own love for him which made him kiss me harder.

He whimpered breathlessly as he buried his head in my neck, and I felt his grip tighten around me as his body shuddered with his own release.

The vague sensation of someone nuzzling my neck woke me up slowly. I popped one eye open, and saw those beautiful blue eyes I loved so much.

"Morning sleepy head," Collin said softly.

"Mmm…good morning," I closed my eye again, and scooted closer to him. He had been waking me up every two hours like the doctor instructed, effectively making me tired beyond belief. I wasn't ready to get up just yet, but I knew Hayley need to be tended too.

"I'm sorry to do this as soon as you wake up but I think we need to talk," he said quietly. My heart sank in the pit of my stomach as soon as the words fell from his lips. Did he regret? Oh god he regretted it. Was he going to tell me he made a mistake? Did he realize he didn't feel the same way about me?

My face must have shown my feelings because he immediately took me in his arms, and his voice became frantic.

"No, no B, what is it? Talk to me," he pushed anxiously. Traitor tears were pooling in my eyes.

"Do you…never mind, it's not important," I said trying to push him away.

"Angel, with all due respect…don't give me that shit, and tell me. Please?" he pleaded, keeping a firm grip on me.

I huffed, "Do you…regret?" I asked hesitantly looking at my hands in my lap, and to my surprise he laughed.

"What? No…B, look at me please?" He lifted my chin with a finger, and stared into my eyes intently, "…Angel…sweetheart, my love, it never even crossed my mind. I don't regret anything. I love you, and I've been waiting to show you just how much I truly do for a long time," he kissed my forehead, and I relaxed immediately, "No, I woke up this morning, and went to check up on Hayley."

I straitened up at once. My little girl…was she alright?

"She was already awake but…she won't come out of her room. She keeps saying her daddy won't leave her alone. I tried B, I tried everything, and nothing worked. She doesn't want to leave her bed at all. I even tried coaxing her into sleeping in here with you but she won't budge. I don't know what to do," he said, and it was apparent in his features how it worried him.

"I'll go see her, thank you." I made a motion to get up but he kept a firm grip on me.

"B, I think Hayley needs more help than you can give her," he said.

"What do you mean?" I asked looking at him with concern. Did he think I was unfit to take care of my child?

"Please, don't take this the wrong way, but I think she needs a *child* psychologist," he murmured. I relaxed a little because unfortunately this wasn't a surprise to me, I had thought of it before.

"I know you can't be expected to do this on your own, Angel. Just because you are a psychologist doesn't mean you can handle the situation, and her emotional outbursts. You can't just stop living to take care of your child. Don't think for a second that you *can't* help her at all that's not true, you absolutely can. You're a wonderful mother, but I can't expect you to do this on your own. You owe this to Hayley, and to yourself; it'll give you some help too," he took my hand, and kissed it.

I bowed my head in shame, and nodded. I knew he was right. I should have done that the first time around, but when she didn't show any signs of trauma, I thought she was going to be fine. I was wrong, and could slap my self for this.

"I'll find a doctor," I whispered shakily.

CHAPTER 23

It was the end of the week when two very important events occurred in our household. I say *our* household because since we came home last week I have been to my house on only two occasions to pick up some clothes. I was afraid to leave them alone, and fortunately for me B refused to let me leave...and believe me I was not fucking complaining. Mika either, she was over the moon to have the house to her self especially since Riley got his head out of his ass, and asked her out.

Today was Friday, and Hayley was scheduled to attend her first therapy session with Dr. Annie Ross, and B decided it would do her good to also see a professional of her own.

The plan for today was to pick up Hayley from my mother's since B had her first appointment this afternoon, and we would meet her at Dr. Ross's office.

My mother agreed to babysit for us since I was also busy filing my paper work for my application to the Federal Bureau of Investigation office of New York. I still had a few weeks of vacation days banked from the precinct so I cashed those in effectively pushing back my release date. Some time off would not hurt.

B was pissed when I told her Captain Broadway fired me, and even more pissed when I told her to expect a call from him. She went on, and on that I didn't deserve that, and when Ed called to tell her she was being sacked too, she just blew up on him. When I told her about the offer Broadway gave me, she folded...a little. She was still furious with me for not telling her this information when I got to the hospital. Though she was glad Ed was going to give her good references so she could search for a new job. Her doctor asked her to stay home for a month or so before starting her search for employment, and since she was with me all week, all I have been doing was beg for her to forgive me…and I was still working on that.

After she told Hayley she would be seeing a doctor for, what we found out was her night terrors, we sat her down, and B explained that she was going to talk to a kid's doctor. Hayley's face had gone pale until B assured her that this doctor wasn't the type who gave shots or sour-tasting medicine. This was a doctor who would just talk with her. Hayley had seemed okay with that explanation, but in true child-like form, waited until I got her in the car, and on the way to the appointment when she finally became nervous enough to ask questions.

"Is the doctow a boy ow giwl?"

"A girl," I explained, "Her name is Dr. Annie, remember?" Traffic was hell, and I was trying so hard not to curse at someone or flip them the fuck off, because the kid in the back seat would no doubt bankrupt me.

I glanced in my rear-view mirror as Hayley nodded, "And no shots?"

I grinned as her eyes found mine in the mirror, "No shots."

"Why does she want to talk to me?"

I took a deep breath, "She wants to see if maybe you want to talk to her."

"About what?" she asked.

"Just different things…." I explained vaguely. What was I supposed to say? She wants to talk to you about how your prick of a father hit, and raped your mother in front of you, and took you hostage at your own daycare. Nope, couldn't say that. Just thinking about it was making me wish he was still alive so I could kill him all over again.

"Like home…your family…your friends…your feelings, and if you're happy or sad. If something is on your heart…"

She looked puzzled, "On my heawt?"

I smiled softly. That was what my mother always said when something was on her mind, that *something is on her heart,* but how to explain that to a little girl?

"Yes, if something or someone is making you happy or sad…or maybe even mad, and you're thinking about it all the time or if there's something you really, really want to talk about. That means it's on your heart," I explained as best as I could.

She seemed to understand this. She was quiet then, just staring out the window as we made our way down the street. Finally, she whispered, "Collin?"

"Hmm?"

"Is something on youw heawt?" she sighed.

"Lots of things are on my heart," I whispered as I stopped at the traffic light.

"Like what?"

"You're on my heart," I smiled in the rear view mirror. I could see her beautiful green eyes reflecting from the backseat.

"Why?" she asked quietly, "Because I make you happy? Ow I make you sad?" her voice was so sweet, and soft, and all I wanted to do was park the car, and hug her.

"Because you make me happy Hayley, you're such a sweet little girl," her smile was breathtaking, and I was reminded once again how very much she looked like her mother.

"I have stuff on my heawt," she murmured softly, her features creased with concentration as she stared out the window again.

"That's okay," I encouraged, trying desperately to hide the concern in my voice, "You should tell Dr. Annie all about it."

After finally navigating us through traffic, and finding a parking space, I grasped Hayley's hand after letting her out of her seat, and led her toward the entrance of the office. B was already waiting for us, her hair in a messy bun, and nervously fidgeting. Even in an acute state of anxiety she was still the most beautiful woman I'd ever laid eyes upon, dressed in a simple blue tank top, jeans, and sneakers.

"Sorry," I muttered as I glanced at my watch, "Traffic was terrible. We aren't late are we?" I asked, "How was your appointment?"

"No, no…right on time," she smiled at me just a brief grin but enough to cause butterflies to erupt in my stomach, even after all this time with her, though not all that long, she still made my insides twist. Unfortunately, it broke my heart to see the anxiety etched upon her perfect face.

"It was alright…it's just strange to be sitting on the other side of the desk if you get what I mean," she laughed nervously. I hugged her shoulders to try, and relax the tension I could feel emanating from her.

"I understand. Relax Angel you're more nervous than your daughter," I whispered under my breath, we were still standing on the sidewalk. "Are you sure about this? I could just wait for you in the car or at a coffee shop, and you could call me when you're done?" I said. I didn't feel like I should be here. Don't get me wrong, I wanted to be there for both of them, but this was a family matter, and I wasn't. I was just the boyfriend.

B looked at me with hurt in her eyes, "Do you want to go? Because, it's alright if you do, but…" she hesitated, biting her lower lip, "I would really feel better if you were there with me," she finished, and stared into my face.

"No I don't want to go, I just didn't want to over step my boundaries. Of course I'll stay with you," I said with a smile.

She took Hayley by the hand before flashing me a sheepish smile. Hayley grabbed my hand with her other free one. She gazed up at each of us, her eyes apprehensive, and unsure. We both smiled down at her as I reassured her that this was going to be a good thing. Over the little girl's head, my eyes locked with B's before her face melted into a heart-stopping smile when she mouthed, "Thank you," and I smiled in return. Hand-in-hand, we walked into the lobby of the doctor's office. It was beautiful, and colorful. Hayley didn't know where to look. The walls where yellow, and blue, toys were scattered all over, and the furniture was white, it really looked like a children's place.

As it turns out, Dr. Annie was a psychologist who was also a play therapist. I had absolutely no idea what that meant, but B did. She explained to both of us that Dr. Annie was going to use toys, and other fun activities to encourage Hayley to tell if something was bothering her. Hayley quickly replied that she had stuff 'on her heart' she wanted to talk about. B looked at me with a puzzled expression, and I said I would explain later.

Dr. Annie was a petite blonde-haired waif who didn't look old enough to buy alcohol. But she was professional and polite as she welcomed all of us into her office. B introduced me as her boyfriend, making me uneasy. I realized it wasn't nearly enough for me, but that was a thought saved for later. She made sure to let the doctor know that it was important to her daughter, and her self that I was involved in every aspect of her therapy, and I *wanted* to be involved as much as B would let me. Hayley's hands remained clutched in ours as Dr. Annie gave us a tour of the facility.

She led us into a small room adjacent her office. The room had a long table, chairs, and on the wall was a large one-way mirror giving us a complete view of her office or playroom. Dr. Annie explained that B, and I would be allowed to watch but not hear the therapy sessions, and I couldn't deny the relief that flowed through me, and through B's eyes when we realized we could actually see what was happening in that room. Hayley was fascinated by the mirror room, but mostly because of the toys she could see through the glass. Dr. Annie explained that B, and I would be waiting in this room while she played with her in the playroom.

"Collin and mommy can't go with me?" Hayley whispered her eyes wide, and fearful. She gripped my hand a little tighter.

"They can today," Dr. Annie replied with a smile, "I'd love to show them the playroom. But after today your mother and Collin will be waiting for you in the mirror room. Remember, they'll be able to see everything we do, and they'll be right there when we're finished playing."

I saw Hayley's eyes flicker to her mother, who nodded, and smiled sweetly down to her, a silent reminder that everything was going be just fine, that this would be fun for her. Dr. Annie then pointed out the restrooms, and encouraged us to take her prior to each session.

"Hayley?" Dr. Annie kneeled in front of her, "We're all going into my office now. You'll probably call it the playroom. There will be lots of toys, and you are welcome to play with any of them. Today, while you play, I'm going to have a talk with your mother, and Collin," Hayley nodded in understanding, and Dr. Annie continued, "I want you to know that I'm so glad you're here today, and anything you tell me while we're in the playroom is private. Do you know what that means?" she asked.

"Like a secwet?" Hayley asked with a whisper.

Dr. Annie nodded enthusiastically, "It means you can tell me anything you want, and I can't share it with your mom or with Collin. It's just between us. The only time I can tell them anything private is if I think you might hurt yourself or someone else, and I won't talk to them without telling you first. From time to time, I will speak with your mother, and Collin to let them know how we're doing, but I can't tell them anything we talk about. Do you understand?"

"Yes," she replied softly.

"Good," Dr. Annie continued with a smile, "Now, if there's ever a time you prefer your mom and Collin not watch us play, then I'll ask them to wait in another room, one without a mirror. Do you think that'd be okay with your mom?"

The doctor looked up at B, and I realized she was asking her thoughts on the matter. Personally, I wasn't thrilled with the idea, but we were going to have to trust this woman, and it wasn't really my place to say anything about it. After looking at me with probably the same concern in her eyes than mine, B nodded.

"Wonderful," she glanced back at Hayley, "Do you have any questions at all?"

She still seemed hesitant but said no as Dr. Annie smiled, and led us to the connecting room. Hayley's eyes lit up when she saw the big white and pink castle in the corner of the room, and we noticed her obvious delight as her eyes scanned the rest of the room. Various toys were placed around the room, along with a child-size table, and chairs. A bop clown stood in the corner, various stuffed animals, and small musical instruments littered the shelves.

"Hayley, go ahead, and check out the toys while I speak with your mother and Collin alright?" Dr. Annie said with a playful tone.

Hayley looked to both of us, and we nodded in encouragement. She headed straight to the castle, and began playing with the dolls. We all sat down together on the sofa, and chair opposite where the toys were. We talked about what Dr. Annie was going to do during those sessions, and all the specifics we, well mostly B, needed to take care of. When we left the office, Hayley was in a good mood contrary to the emotional state she was in at the beginning of the week so I proposed we take a walk, and get ice cream. Hayley squealed loudly, and asked to sit on my shoulders which I obliged; that kid had me wrapped around her little finger.

On our way back to the car B and Hayley's eyes lit up when we passed a flower shop. I couldn't help but smile as they pulled me into the florist, and looked at all the flowers in all the different colors. B explained to her that flowers didn't come in only one or two colors, but hundreds of shades, and Hayley was eating up every single shred of information her mother was saying. I leaned down next to Hayley when B walked farther away from us.

"Hey, why don't we pick out a flower for your mom?" I murmured in her ear. She giggled as she nodded excitedly, and pulled me toward a display of freshly cut roses. Her eyes were bright with excitement as she looked at all the roses, and plucked a yellow one from a vase.

"This one," she whispered, and then I watched in amazement as she ran to B's side. She pulled on the leg of her jeans until she finally looked down at her. She gasped in surprise as Hayley handed her the rose. She kneeled down, and softly kissed her cheek as I paid the florist for the flower. She could have charged me a thousand bucks for that single yellow rose, and I wouldn't have cared less. The smile on Hayley's face was priceless.

As we got to her mother's car, I helped Hayley climb in her seat, and when I turned around B was standing next to her door, staring down at the yellow rose. Loose strands of her hair were blowing in the breeze, and her smile was soft as she gazed down at the flower. I'd never seen anyone look more angelic.

I opened the door for her as she finally looked up at me. Our eyes locked, and very slowly she walked the two step distance between us. Clutching her rose in her hand, she rose on her tiptoe, and placed a kiss on my lips. My eyes closed as her soft lips lingered on my skin.

"Thank you for the flower…I'm still upset with you though. Don't think this gets you off the hook Mister," she whispered softly against my mouth. I had to resist the urge to wrap my arms around her body as she pulled away; I just never wanted her away from me.

I chuckled, "You're welcome, and I'll make it up to you I promise…B,

Captain Broadway said I could still attend the annual NYPD charity event since I already purchased the tickets, and I'd love to take you," I asked hesitantly. I half expected her to tell me off but the sweetest smile crept across her face.

"I'd love to go with you."

CHAPTER 24

D r. Annie was doing wonders with Hayley, though she hadn't spoken about Brian yet, she was doing better at home. Her nightmares still plagued her sleep, but at least during the day she was mostly back to normal. Two weeks passed since our first visit, and Collin was truly a God send to us. He came to her appointments every time, and took us for ice cream afterward. Hayley was head over heels for him, and so was I.

Collin went back to his house a week, and some days following the daycare situation after some convincing I might add. I didn't want him to go back home, I loved having him with us, but what's the point in paying for a house if you're never there? I gave him a key to my house though, so he could come by any time he wanted. I was still a little irked with him, and I made it a purpose to ignore him as much as I could handle. But one look in those baby blues of his was making my task nearly impossible! The NYPD Charity Ball was tomorrow, and since I was home alone I opted for a nice relaxing bath. The Ball was stressing me out like you wouldn't believe. I had never been to something of that magnitude, and I didn't know what to expect. Who was going to be there? What was I suppose to where? Would I know everyone there or was it all of New York's finest?

Hayley was currently visiting with Collin's mother, and I had already secured a babysitter for tomorrow. I couldn't ask Claire since the whole Haywood family was going to be at the Charity event.

With all those thoughts in my head I wrapped a towel around me, stepped out of the tub, and headed for my room when I heard knocking downstairs. I stepped on the last stair when my favorite sound in the world came to my ears.

"B? It's me, open up please I forgot my keys," Collin screamed through the door.

"Collin?" I asked. Okay, now I knew that was stupid.

"Yes," he answered slowly...Ass, "And this is a door," he said after knocking on it again. "Now are you going to open it or are we going to keep talking through it?" he asked.

Oh yeah. See? I knew I loose IQ points around that man...Sad.

"Shut up, I'm coming," I laughed as I walked toward the door. Then I realized what I had said, and started to cut him off before he could put a word in.

"And don't you dare say that's what..." I began, but that was as far as I got before I pulled the door all the way open, and got a look at the sight before me.

"What..." I breathed or gasped because I honestly couldn't tell you what came out of my mouth. There he was. Right before my eyes, and driving me out of my mind! Again.

Wet Collin...

Wet, rain-drenched Collin....

Wet, rain-drenched, just-came-from-his-afternoon-jog Collin...

I had to hold my breath, and close my eyes to keep from embarrassing the crap out of myself, and moaning. When I regained some kind of control, I slowly opened my eyes again to let myself drink in the sight of him. Still didn't work! His hair was drenched by the rain making them look darker than usual, and falling onto his forehead. The rain dripped from his face, and over his lips before it traveled down over his bare shoulders, his arms, and across his tank-clad chest, and stomach. That wet, black shirt of sin hugged tightly against his body like a second skin, revealing every single god darn muscle, and making my tongue throb with the urge to lick him. His black and white basketball shorts were hung low on his hips due to the weight of the water, and I swear I was now paralyzed.

My insides felt like they were on fire just being close to him. Fighting with everything in me, I removed my eyes from his body, and slowly brought them back up. I felt myself smile as my heart skipped.

"Fuck…" he whispered.

The sound of his gruff voice brought me back…bad idea! I should've just kept my eyes on the floor, but of course a decision like that would require common sense, and right now that was so far out of the window it wasn't even funny. When I finally did look up at his face, I had to tighten my grip on the door handle. His eyes were squeezed shut, his lips were pressed tightly together, and his head was thrown back and slightly shaking back, and forth. When his Adam's apple slowly rose, and lowered with his deep swallow, I smiled a little. Did the fact that I was affecting him this way make me feel good? Hell yes! I felt like I could take on the world in that moment.

The fact that we've only said maybe two words to each other since I opened this door was not intentional or forgotten. I just couldn't think of anything to say. What was I supposed say to the man of your dreams standing on your doorstep soaking wet? 'Fuck me up against my door'. I don't think so. Although…..nah…won't work…but I had to say something… anything!

"Rain," oh, dear lord…psychological degree my butt. I had to shake my own head at myself.

"Towel," he answered.

Okay, so maybe I was not the only temporarily dumb one here for the moment.

"Ugh?" Then again…

Instead of answering with words, I followed his eyes as they traveled up my bare calves, and thighs…right up to the bottom hem of my short, white towel. Oh right…towel. I should have been shocked or embarrassed, cowering behind the door, but instead I leaned back against the doorframe, crossed my legs at the ankles, and folded my arms over my chest. I had never felt more confident, and cocky but exposed, and safe at the same time. Those feelings, and the fact that his fists just balled up by his hips while his eyes narrowed on me also helped the 'cocky' bit do a little side step, and flip off the rest of the world.

"I just came to see you before I head back home. Do you have a towel?" he said with a glint in his eyes after looking at the puddle of water at his feet.

"Hum, yeah upstairs, you know where they are…wouldn't want you to catch a cold now do we," I didn't even try to hide my disappointment.

"Yeah," he muttered. He looked down at his feet before bringing his eyes back up to mine. The bright blue gleam was almost blinding, and absolutely breathtaking. I felt the breath slowly swoosh out of my body. He grabbed my hands before squeezing them, letting them go after rubbing my fingers for a moment, and turning toward the stairs.

Every fiber of my being was yelling at me to stop him. A huge part of me knew that if I didn't stop him now, I would spontaneously combust. I mean I couldn't stay mad at him forever now could I? He said he was sorry like a million times already.

I tried to call his name, but my throat seemed to be against us. I slapped the hell out of my stupidity; I mean this man loved me. He didn't exactly mean to keep things from me. Though, getting fired would have something I definitely wanted to know from the get go, he was just trying to protect me until I could handle the news a little better. So I tried again.

"Collin?" I called. I froze when he did at the sound of my voice, and felt my heart stop when he began to turn back toward me.

"I'm…" but stopped and pulled my bottom lip into my mouth, and bit down hard, not knowing what to do or say. I knew I should apologize for ignoring him; it *was* a little too harsh considering the circumstances. I knew better than that.

"Fuck it," he groaned, before closing the gap between us, placing my face between his hands, and crashing his lips down onto mine. I sighed against his lips as my eyes closed, my knees wobbled, and my lips burned at the contact. My arms went around his neck as we backed up, and stopped when my back smashed against the wall in the hallway. Pictures, and mirrors shook, and something or another fell off of the hall table.

I let out a moan, and felt him smile against my lips before he began kissing me in a way that would undo me faster than I could have imagined. His mouth opened to me as I was sucking on his bottom lip, and when our tongues touched, it was like a massive eruption of moans, groans, and sexy-as-all-hell growls. The week of built up frustration, the arguments, and the want came crashing down on us in that moment, and we attacked each other's mouths with abandon, and it was complete, and utter bliss. It started slow, sensual, and powerful, before turning into something that left my lungs burning, and me panting, making my head spin even more…and not from the lack of oxygen. The mere taste of him felt like velvet.

"Angel…" he moaned. His hands moved from my face down to my bare shoulders, and over my arms before settling on my hips. I gripped onto his still wet tank by his neck, enjoying the feel of the water as it ran down my hands, and pulled his body as close to mine as it could possibly get. When I felt myself being lifted off of my feet, my thighs immediately wrapped around his hips, and held on for dear life. One hand was left on my hip while his other traveled up, and sprawled out on my side. His hands left a trail of goose bumps wherever they touched. His body was literally molded to mine up against the wall, and there was no mistaking that I was not the only one enjoying this. Jesus Christ Shepherd of Jedidiah!

Without warning, his lips began to move away from mine, and I had the sudden urge to slap him back to his senses. His hot forehead gently rested against mine, and I closed my eyes, and listened to his labored breathing.

"I'm so sorry B, I really am…I should have told you about it but I…" he started, but I interrupted him quickly.

"Collin, forget about it. I know why you did it, and I appreciate it more than you know. I shouldn't have over reacted like I did. Just promise me next time something this important happens you won't keep it from me?" I said, and he nodded in agreement.

With that said, he brought his lips to mine, and kissed me so softly, running his hands down my sides pulling me to him. Our lips began to move in unison again, increasing the urgency, and finally his tongue entered my mouth, exploring, and tasting me with great need.

I pulled him closer, wrapping my arms around his neck. Every desire I've felt for him was coming out ten fold…no longer upset or wanting to hold anything back, I kissed him with passion, with fervor, and my need for him to touch me this way was far greater than the annoyance I had for him before.

The kiss grew with more heated passion, and almost roughly, he pushed off the wall, and walked us to the living room his hands roaming my thighs. I swung my hips against his, earning groans, and moans from him.

"Holy fuck B, are you trying to give me a heart attack?" he groaned. Feeling sexy, and frisky, I couldn't help but tease.

"Why no, Mr. Haywood, why would you ever think that?" I asked innocently. His eyes darkened, and a much more serious tone fell on his features.

He sat me down on the sofa, laying my back against the arm rest, and lowered himself. His mouth reaching my thighs, he kissed the exposed area under the hem of my towel, and parted my knees. His tongue darted out, and created a hot, wet line up to my inner thigh where he gave my delicate skin a light nibble with his teeth.

"Mmm…you're truly delectable. I've missed that taste," he said, and he lifted himself with one knee on the sofa in between my thighs, allowing me to wrap my legs around him, and bring him closer.

"What are you doing to me B?" His arms wrapped around my waist, and his kiss came down on my mouth with a vengeance. He rocked in between my legs, pressing against my core, right where I wanted us to join so badly.

He was panting, kissing my neck, my cheeks, my lips, my throat. His fingers approached my chest, and began undoing my towel, so I began pulling his shirt up. He easily pulled the towel right from under me, and slowly took the shirt off of him, his chest finally revealed to me. He paused kissing me, taking a long hard look at me, and lowering his mouth to my breasts.

My hands ran through his hair, holding his head there, loving the feeling of his hot breath, his tongue, and his soft hair tickling my bare skin.

CHAPTER 25

This amazing woman was mine, and I could scream it to the world. When I pulled the towel from underneath her, and our bodies touched she moaned, and I groaned, and pushed her further against the couch before my lips found hers. I kissed her with all of the pent up passion, and frustration I had in me, and she threw it back at me, full force. Our tongues clashed, and our chests pressed together, and when I pressed against her hips she groaned against my lips, and moved them against mine.

I pulled my lips away from hers, and began kissing down her body. I licked, and kissed her neck and chest before pulling one of her glorious breast into my mouth. I ran my tongue around the sensitive skin, and watched as it hardened in pleasure.

She moaned, and ran her fingernails over my back, and arms. Her fingers dipped into each divot as she grazed me with reverence before her hand finally reached its destination in my hair. She gripped it, pulled it, and moaned...my fucking world stopped. I groaned loudly against her breast, and she hissed when I pulled her skin between my teeth. Her hands moved again reaching my shorts, pulling at the strings to loosen them, and began the motions as she worked me. She stroked from the base to the head, and down again before lightly trailing her nails over.

"Fuck!" I breathed against her neck. My hands gripped her ass, and a long sexy moan escaped her lips when I lifted one of her legs onto my bent one, and entered a finger deep inside her. When she started to move her hips with the motion of my hand I became even harder over the sexy fucking noises coming from her.

"Oh, god Coll…" she whispered. When her moans became louder, and her hip thrusting harder, I kissed her again, and she wrapped her other leg around me. Her hips began grinding harder, and my fingers were drenched. Her moans grew when my thumb started teasing her center, and I pulled her bottom lip between my teeth sucking on it, stretching out her delicious moans. Her hand suddenly tightened on me.

"Fuck," I moaned against her mouth. She grabbed my hair tighter with the other hand, and dove her tongue into my mouth to silence me. Her hand continued to work the shit out of me while she rode my fingers. Her nails dug into my scalp, and I felt her beginning to clench around my fingers. Her head was thrown back, and her mouth was slightly parted in her fast pants, and breathing.

I quickly removed myself before she was done, effectively earning a glare from my beautiful woman. I chuckled, stood up, and removed my shorts, letting them drop to the floor. Seeing what I was doing B stood on her knees, and immediately pulled me back to her.

I spun around as she pinned me to the couch to climb on my lap, and trusted her hips into mine. I buried myself in her, and we both moaned loudly. Our breathing was matched, and we were panting like animals. I was sweating like a fucking pig too, but I honestly couldn't bring my self to care. I lifted her higher bringing her face level with mine, and kissed *my* woman. She sighed against my lips, and wrapped her thighs around my waist tighter than before, pressing her wet lips against mine. While still kissing her, I moaned into her mouth when she sank down onto me again, and I was finally and fully inside of her.

"Oh, God," she choked out.

"Don't worry, he's watching," I teased, earning a smile from her.

B's head flew back, and she began slowly sliding up, and down, swirling her hips in a circular motion that almost made me fucking drop the bomb right then, and there. She sat up, grabbed the back of my head, and pulled my lips to hers, silencing my moans. I tightened my grip on her hips, and wrapped one arm completely around her, bringing her body flush against mine as I began thrusting into her deeper.

"Ooh fuck!" she yelled, effectively surprising me. My woman wasn't one for cursing. I laughed a little kissing her deeper, and groaned out her full name against her lips as she wrapped her arms around my shoulders, and rode me on her own. I fisted my hands on the couch next to me, and when I tilted my hips forward I found the magic spot. B screamed against my lips, and bit on my bottom one when I felt the walls begin to clench around me. As she screamed, my hand tightened around her waist as I felt my own release approaching, and began thrusting harder, and faster.

She started to scream louder, but I grabbed her wet hair, and bit into her neck at an attempt to silence the scream that was escaping as her body shivered, and convulsed. My laughter was cut off by my own moan as I was close to release.

With a final thrust, and hair being damn near ripped out, her body shivered, and her muffled moans increased with screams bouncing off the walls. I pulled her flush against me as I continued to thrust within her, against her spasms. Her intense tightening around me, the sound of my name from her mouth, seeing her writhe above me was all my ending.

My face was quickly placed in the crook of her sweat-glistened neck as I finally ended. My body locked along with my grip on her, and she pressed me further into the sofa as the volume of my groan increased. Her voice and breathing was sparse, and shuddered as she licked the outside of my mouth, and moaned when I kissed her back, hard. She tightened her legs around me, and ran her nails up, and down my shoulders as my shudders continued to rock through me from the biggest fucking orgasm of my life. She continued to kiss me softly against numb lips as our breathing, and heart rates slowed.

"I can't feel my legs," she laughed, sounding a little drunk…loving it.

"I don't even remember what legs are right about now," I replied. Especially since the wobbly ones sticking from under her, couldn't possibly be mine. She laughed again into my neck, and I grabbed her towel from the floor, and wrapped it around her back before I walked us back into her shower.

Mika pulled me through the threshold of the flower store on Saturday morning. I was not willing to do this with her, but she insisted that I needed to kiss ass for my actions, and for that, I needed her *expertise*.

The staff noticed her, and immediately paled. Obviously, the flower shop staff was well-acquainted with my loud-mouthed sister.

"I need Stephan!" she snapped at nobody in particular, and I watched with fascination as the workers scampered in various directions. Moments later, a tall gentleman appeared. He was dressed impeccably in a white business suit with a purple tie. He was very tall, and very French. His hair was a light strawberry blond, and very tousled.

"My beautiful Mikaylah," Stephan welcomed with an air kiss to both her cheeks. Then his eyes fell to me, and I shuffled uncomfortably as his brown eyes roamed up, and down my body. Seems like Stephan was also very gay, and I cleared my throat nervously.

"He's straight, Stephan," Mika smirked, causing the florist to pout.

"Of course he is," the man lamented with just a trace of a French accent, "What can I do for the two of you?"

"This is my brother. He wants to seriously kiss up to the woman he loves. Help him?" Mika said.

"Ah…" Stephan appraised me longingly, and I rolled my eyes as he clapped his hands, "So we need beautiful flowers. Tell me, what is her name?"

"Belladonna," I replied softly.

"Ah, Belladonna…." Stephan sighed, "Tell me about the Beautiful Woman while we have a look around."

So I did. I told this very gay man all about the girl who has stolen my heart, and made my world a beautiful place. I told him about Hayley, and how the two of them have completely changed my life.

"So help him woo her, Stephan," Mika smirked as she pushed the buttons of her Blackberry. I flashed a look of annoyance her way, and she flipped me the bird.

"We need beautiful flowers for the Beautiful Woman," Stephan surmised as we made our way through the multi-color stems. They all looked the same to me. I traced the bloom of a red rose, and Mika groaned slapping my fingers away from them.

"Don't you dare pick a red rose, be creative for God's sake," she growled under her breath just as Stephan dragged me to a display of purple flowers.

"Those are…pretty?" I asked self-consciously, because God knows apparently I needed to be creative.

"Ah lavender roses…" Stephan swooned as he brought one out of the vase, and then he began reciting flower facts like a possessed man. "The unique beauty of the lavender rose has captured many hearts, and imaginations. With their fantastical appearance, lavender roses are a perfect symbol of enchantment and royalty. The lavender rose is also traditionally used to express feelings of love at first sight."

Love at first sight. That sounded…perfect.

"Perfect," I replied, very proud of my self for choosing such an ideal flower, "I'll take a dozen."

"He'll take three!" Mika snapped, and Stephan clapped his fabulous hands.

I had one dozen delivered directly to B's house, and brought the others with me to drop them off at home. I spent the rest of the day showering, and getting everything ready for the ball tonight. I left the house in the afternoon to pick up the babysitter. Her name was Katie, a small sixteen years old with fire red hair, and freckles.

Mika was at B's house to help her get ready for the Ball, and after dropping off Katie I went back to mine so I could change into my tuxedo. Of course, I was so god damn nervous I couldn't get the stupid ass bow tie right, so I just left it hanging from my neck. I walked into my lobby, pick up the flowers I got for her, and gingerly placed them on the passenger seat of my truck. I thought of that morning again, and shuttered at the memory. I was never doing that again…at least not with my sister.

I got to B's house with flowers overflowing in my arms. As soon as I opened the door Hayley ran to me, and took my hand to lead me toward the living room, I mentally prepared myself for this night. I hadn't enjoyed this gala in years, and I was determined to have a good time tonight. I deserved it…my Angel *definitely* deserved it…and she deserved to be treated like a lady, and not have some hormonal, sex-starved ex-cop groping her all night. I would be courteous. I would be respectful. I would be a gentleman.

"Mommy looks weal pwetty you know!" Hayley whispered.

"Does she now?"

And then I saw her standing next to the fire place talking with my sister along with the babysitter, and all of my chivalrous ideas were shot to hell. B turned our way, and when her eyes locked with mine, she smiled the most heartbreaking smile, and I was certain I had never seen anything so beautiful in my entire life.

Her dress was ivory satin. Her black hair hung down her bare back in loose waves. My fingers itched to touch the porcelain skin of her exposed back, and I took solace in the fact that I would have her in my arms soon enough.

"Told'ya she was pwetty," Hayley smiled up at me.

"You were right," I grinned at her. I looked back at B, and she was blushing. She literally took my breath away. "She's right," I whispered eagerly, "You look so beautiful, Angel."

"*Those* are beautiful," she smiled shyly. I handed her the lavenders.

"There's no comparison," I said. She took them from me, and Mika took them right out of B's hands.

"I'll take care of these, and then I'm out, I'll see you there." And she was off. B turned to me with a smile.

"You look pretty handsome yourself. Do you need some help with your tie?"

I could only nod as she very carefully and expertly maneuvered the bowtie. Not that I actually watched her handiwork. I couldn't tear my eyes away from her face long enough and frankly at this moment I couldn't give a shit about my tie. This gorgeous woman was going to be on my arm tonight.

In my arms tonight…

"There you go," she smiled sweetly at me. Her fingers softly grazed the lapel of my tux.

"Thank you," I murmured softly as we continued to gaze at each other. I could see Hayley in my peripheral vision with a huge smile on her face along with Katie. B blinked rapidly, and finally broke the spell. She looked down at Hayley.

"Promise to be a good girl with Katie tonight?" she asked her daughter.

"Pwomise," she smiled brightly, and turned to me, "Do you pwomise to dance with mommy? She wants you too."

B groaned, but I couldn't deny her anything. Her eyes flashed to me as her cheeks flushed.

"I promise to dance with your mommy," I vowed before kissing her cheek. She leaned in to kiss me back, planting a big wet kiss on my cheek, and I hugged her. She wrapped her little arms around me, and squeezed.

"I love you princess, and we'll see you in the morning."

"Love you, Collin," she said back, and B leaned down saying good bye to her daughter before giving me another one of her breathtaking, heart stopping smiles. I smiled contently, and offered my hand.

"Are you ready?" I asked.

"Yes," she whispered as she laced her fingers with mine.

"I know it's for a good cause, but I hate these fucking tuxedos," Riley grimaced as he pulled his tie away from his neck. I grunted in agreement. Everyone was laughing, and joyous, and having a great time. Everyone that is, except for me. My beautiful date had been ripped from my arm as soon as we entered the banquet hall.

I glanced over at B, who was sandwiched at the end of the table between my sister, and my mother. She had been the center of attention all night. I had kept them informed about Hayley's progress with the therapist, and my parents loved B and Hayley so much already they kept lavishing her with praise. If she was flustered, she certainly hid it well. Every time I looked at her she was either smiling or laughing or both.

"You've got it bad for B, huh?" Riley chuckled. I tore my eyes away from her just long enough to glare in his direction…and then inspiration struck.

"Why don't you ask my sister to dance?" I asked him, and Riley shot me a disgusted look.

"Why the hell would I do that? You know I hate dancing," he puckered his face.

"Because if you dance with my sister, maybe I can drag B away from my mother, and then *I* can dance with *her*," I explained.

"You want to dance with your mother?" he asked incredulous.

"Damn it, Riley…." I grimaced, "No, I don't want to dance with my mother. I want to dance with B." I was getting impatient with him. He was my best friend but sometimes I would have loved to kick his ass.

He chuckled, "Please. You don't want to *dance* with that girl. You just can't wait to get your hands on her, and dancing is a convenient excuse to touch her in public, without getting arrested for indecent behavior," he laughed even harder when I didn't bother to deny it.

"I don't know what the hell my sister sees in you," I grumbled, which only made him laugh harder.

"Man…you really like this girl," he surmised, "Well, Haywood…here's a novel concept for you. Why don't you just fucking ask her to dance?" he said with a raised eyebrow.

On cue, Jonathan Cross, an intern at the precinct, appeared out of thin air. I watched in quiet fury as he walked right up to B, and offered his hand to her. Irrational jealousy coursed through my body. It only subsided when B's eyes flashed to mine. Cross glanced in my direction, and nodded politely before promptly slinking away apologizing. With conviction I stood up, and headed for the end of the table. B's eyes had followed me from the moment I rose from my seat, and our eyes remained locked until I reached her.

"I'm stealing my date back," I announced firmly, never breaking my gaze from hers. A small grin crossed her features as I offered my hand to her. I ignored my sister's, and mother's smiling faces as B placed her hand in mine. Without another word, I led her to a quiet corner of the dance floor.

"What took you so long?" she asked quietly as I pulled her into my arms. My fingers pressed softly against the bare skin of her lower back. Her skin was so soft, and just that simple touch caused my traitorous body to react to her close proximity.

"You seemed engrossed in conversation with them," I murmured as I gazed into her face, "They adore you," I said.

B smiled softly, "Mika is adorable, and your mother is wonderful. But still…I would rather have been dancing with you. We promised Hayley, after all…"

"We did promise Hayley," I agreed with a nod, "She'll be happy to know I made good on my promise," I said smiling.

B laughed lightly as the song changed to a soft tune, and our bodies instinctively moved closer together. I pressed her closer to me, and she sighed softly. Running my fingers through her hair, I admired the soft texture of the silky curls.

"You're the most beautiful woman in this room," I whispered. Her face flushed crimson, and I couldn't resist brushing my finger along her cheek. She sighed as she leaned into my touch. Our bodies swayed in rhythm to the violin. It was pure ecstasy the combined sensations of her flowery scent, and the touch of her creamy skin. I hummed softly as my lips ghosted across her cheek, and she trembled in my arms. She sighed, and nuzzled my neck as we swayed to the music; she felt so good in my arms. Her small frame pressed against me, and we molded perfectly to each other just like corresponding puzzle pieces finally finding their homes.

It was frightening.

It was overpowering.

It was heaven.

It was everything I'd ever wanted but never knew it actually existed.

CHAPTER 26

"B before you go, I was wondering if you would consider dancing with an old man?"

"Dad…" Collin began to argue, and I couldn't help but giggle.

"It's okay," I assured him, "I'd love to dance with you, Mr. Haywood…"

"Charles, please…" he grinned at me before he looked back to his exasperated son.

"I promise, Collin, just a quick dance. I've hardly had the chance to speak with her, what with your mother, and sister monopolizing her all night long. Go say goodnight to your mother…we won't be long," Charles said sternly. Collin's eyes flickered to mine, and I almost laughed at his infuriated expression.

His father's voice was low, and soothing when he said, "*You* get to take her home son." And with that gentle reminder, Collin's face softened.

"I'll give you just one quick dance, dad," he muttered as he turned on his heels, and stalked off in search of his mother. Charles laughed as he offered his hand to me.

"He's very protective of you, and Hayley. It shows in the way he looks, and talks about the two of you," he mused as we waltzed. "That's not a side of Collin we see very often."

"I'm so embarrassed, sometimes we forget we're not alone," I admitted shyly. I glanced over at their table, and saw Collin gazing at me. His mother was looking between the two of us, watching him watching me, and there was a look of ecstatic joy on her face.

"Don't be," Charles murmured softly, "I was young once upon a time. I remember when I was unable to keep my hands off Claire. I still have problems keeping my hands off her," he shrugged.

I laughed in spite of my humiliation. "This is all new to us," I said, and shot him a teasing smile. I glanced once again at the table, and couldn't keep from laughing when I saw Collin staring a hole through us, impatiently tapping his foot on the dance floor. With a flourish of a violin, the sweet waltz ended, and I could see him already making his way to our side. Charles noticed this as well, and laughed as he kissed my hand.

"It seems my time is up. You *are* lovely," he smiled softly, "Thank you my dear."

"Thank *you*," I grinned just as Collin grabbed my hand. He abruptly told his father goodnight, and led me back to the table. Claire hugged me tightly, and Mika smirked behind her shoulder. Mika was sitting on Riley's lap, and they both looked sufficiently plastered.

"Call me," Mika mouthed, Collin and I both wished everyone goodnight as we made our way through the banquet hall, and out into the cool New York air. Collin handed the valet our ticket (along with what looked like a fifty dollar bill), and muttered that we were in a hurry. As the young guy ran like the wind toward the parking garage, Collin took off his jacket, and placed it around my shoulders. Grateful, I snuggled into its warmth until he stepped behind me, wrapping his arms around my waist, and pulling me against his chest. His nose traced a line along my neck, and I trembled as his breath tickled my skin.

"Cold?" he whispered against my ear.

"No," I murmured breathlessly.

I was definitely not cold.

"You're shivering." His hands traveled up, and down my arms as he placed a soft kiss behind my ear. He brushed my hair over one shoulder, and moved the collar of his tux jacket, allowing him to trail his lips across the side of my neck making me tremble even more.

"I wonder why?" I said. Instinctively, I leaned back against him, and I could feel the proof of his arousal pressing against me. He moaned in my ear as he pushed forward, and I reciprocated by pushing against him again.

"I have *got* to get you to the room," he groaned lowly just as the valet appeared with the truck.

The drive to our hotel was filled with sexual tension, and excitement. My mind conjured all kinds of explicit, R-rated images of what might happen when we finally made it to our hotel. He never let go of my hand, and at one point he actually pulled my hand to his face, and kissed it softly brushing my knuckles with his lips.

I was pretty sure I was going to hyperventilate. I had no idea how he could bring such reactions out of me every time he touched me. It wasn't the first time he did, and surprisingly it always felt like it.

With the truck finally parked in the garage, Collin grabbed my hand, and pulled me toward the hotel elevator that brought us the main floor. We hurried as much as we could to settle our reservation, get our key cards, and rushed through the lobby into the second elevator. Thankfully, the operator was nowhere in sight. After pressing the button to the penthouse, he turned to me with a look so hungry that my stomach muscles tightened in anticipation. He was just about to lean in when someone yelled to hold the elevator doors. We jumped apart as an older gentleman, dressed in a black business suit joined us for the ride up.

I sighed a little too dramatically; Collin peered at the man's back with so much annoyance I almost laughed out loud…almost.

"Sir…" the man offered in greeting as he pressed the button for the tenth floor.

Collin only nodded back. I've always loved how men can just greet each other either by name or by just a motion of their chins, and make it look like it's the most ordinary thing in the world.

"It's a beautiful night, isn't it?" the man smiled. His eyes flickered to me, appraising me from head to toe. I shuffled a little bit, and Collin moved closer, wrapping his arm around my waist, and pulling me to his side.

"Yes, it is," he agreed. Soon enough the elevator dinged and we watched the doors opened to our passenger's floor.

"Goodnight," the man grinned, taking one last look at me before exiting. I exhaled a deep breath as the doors shut once again. Collin grasped my hand in his, and I could feel the annoyance of being interrupted flowing through his body.

"Relax buddy, would you?" I teased him.

He just held my hand tighter as I watched the lights flicker on the elevator. The doors finally opened, and Collin pulled me eagerly toward the penthouse doors.

When we entered the room, I went straight to the bathroom, and started filling the giant jetted tub with steaming hot water, and bubbles. The bathtub was huge, and white just like the rest of the room except for the counter top and shelves. They were a rich black ceramic. The mirror mounted on the wall was huge and I checked my reflexion in the mirror, making sure the minimal make up I had was still properly in place. I took off all of my clothes, and wrapped my self in one of the huge white towels. I pulled my hair up in a messy bun on top of my head to make sure I didn't wet them too much. After checking myself in the mirror one last time, I came out of the bathroom just in time to stop Collin from taking off his shoes. I kneeled down in front of him, and untied his laces.

"B?" he asked puzzled.

"Shhh…" I stood, and *very slowly* removed his tie, vest, and button up shirt. I bit my lip, and breathed in deeply when his 'v' was revealed due to his low-slung slacks. His toned chest came into my line of vision, and relaxed as my fingers worked the buttons of his shirt. I had to fight every instinct in me not to lick him. His chin, and neck was then revealed, and leaning in I placed a small kiss on it. He smirked at my obvious ogling, and leaned in to kiss me, but I pushed him back, and continued to undress him. I unzipped his pants, and they fell to a pool around his feet. He stepped out of them, and was only left standing in his black boxer-briefs. I internally groaned, and then pulled him into the bathroom. I removed my towel, and then climbed into the tub, shutting off the running water when it was full enough. I closed my eyes as the hot water began to relax my tight muscles, and let a moan escape. I opened my eyes when I heard Collin take a deep breath, and saw him leaning against the door with his arms folded across his beautiful chest.

"Strip, and get your beautiful butt in this tub, Haywood," I said. He smiled shaking his head while pulling down his boxers. It was my turn to take in a deep breath as I stared at the body of the beautiful God in front of me. He stepped into the tub, and I pulled him toward me, his back on my chest. I ran my fingers through his hair, over his shoulder, and down his chest, and abs. I continued to do this, adding my nails every now, and then earning the most delicious sounds from him. I grabbed the soap next to the side of the tub, and washed all of him that was exposed above the water.

"God B...that feels damn good," he moaned. When I couldn't reach the rest, I made him stand up with me, and I washed the rest of him. I stepped out of the tub, and turned on the hot shower, pulling him inside to get us rinsed off. When we were thoroughly rinsed we stepped out of the shower, and I dried him off, paying extra attention to every inch of his body. When he was thoroughly dried, I dried myself while pushing his busy hands away, and we made our way back into the bedroom. He pulled back the beautiful white covers on the king size bed, and we both climbed in, sighing as the incredibly soft sheets caressed our naked skin.

We made love for hours on a king-sized bed in a five-star hotel with the New York lights shining through the windows, and it was magical. But none of that other crap was needed with Collin. He was more than enough; more than I could ever ask for...wish for, and I was going to make sure he never doubted it.

CHAPTER 27

The rest of the summer passed so quickly I was sure I'd stepped into a time machine. So much had happened in such a short period of time, and it was taking all of us some time to adjust.

Within weeks after the Ball, I asked B to move in with me. To my incredible joy she said yes, but she was a little worried my house wasn't very child proof and the fact that Mika lived with me was a problem. Being the good person she was, my Angel didn't want to kick Mika out, and as much as I loved my sister I didn't want her to live with us. So we agreed I would sell my house to Mika, and move in with B.

But, Belladonna being Belladonna, said we should just get another home, one that was just ours. Hayley was ecstatic while we house shopped. She actually chose the house herself. We were driving around the upper west side looking for an address our realtor gave us when Hayley suddenly screeched for us to stop. I slammed the brakes to the Mercedes certain I hit a cat or something by the way she screamed.

She said to go back because she saw *our* house…and lucky for us, it was for sale too! It was a beautiful blue gray, with white trimmings, and a wrap around porch. The yard was big enough for Hayley to play in without us being afraid of the street traffic.

We moved in three weeks later.

The FBI called me to schedule appointments to have me tested on different matters of experience, education, and knowledge. Exams after exams after exams, they finally took me in. I was Special Agent Haywood

150

of the Federal Bureau of Investigation, and I was damn proud of my self. B and Hayley were jumping all over the house when I gave them the news.

B started looking for work not too long ago when her Doctor gave her the okay. Unfortunately, it wasn't going very well in the criminal department, so she decided to go back to school, and study children psychology. Her experience with Hayley's problems gave her the idea. I was behind her all the way. I had a good job, and I was doing very well on the society scale, and B still had an impressive amount from her divorce, so we were doing just fine.

Dr. Annie was doing wonders with Hayley; she finally talked about what was on her heart, and she no longer had nightmares about *that* day. She was starting to recall some bits, and pieces from the days when B and Brian were still married, and it worried us beyond belief. Dr. Annie said not to worry about it, because as long as she continued acting like her normal self, and talking about it, everything was alright.

I often worked from home instead of at the office when I didn't have to travel. At least that way I could see Hayley and my Angel more often than not. I was in my office just getting off the phone with my partner when B signaled me that Hayley was in bed waiting for me to say good night. I nodded, and made my way to her.

I slowly opened her door, just in case she was already sleeping. When she popped one eye open and saw I was standing at her door she extended her little arms for me. I walked to her bed, and layed down next to her.

"Shouldn't you be sleeping?" I whispered.

"I was waiting fow you. What took you so long?" she whined.

"I'm sorry princess I was on the phone with work, but I'm here now. Give me a hug so you can go to sleep," I said laughing. She lifted her little arms, and wrapped them around my neck as I wrapped my own around her small frame, and hugged her tightly.

"Good night princess, I'll see you in the morning alright!" I patted the blankets around her, and made sure she had her teddy bear.

"Good night!" she yawned.

I stood, closed her light and walked to the door. As I was about to close the door I completely froze at her next words.

"Love you daddy," she said sleepily.

I was in utter shock, but the smile on my face could have fooled anyone.

"I love you too sweetie." I closed her door, and went to our room. I froze again when I entered, and I saw B settled in the middle of our bed, crying. I ran to her right away, if there was something I couldn't stand it was seeing my beautiful Angel crying.

"Angel, what's wrong? What happened?" I said urgently as I cradled her against me.

"I heard..."she pointed to the baby monitor on the night stand, and I understood what she meant. "I heard everything. Collin? Are you..." she hesitated.

"Do you want the honest truth?" I asked her. She nodded slowly after wiping her eyes with her finger tips.

"It's the most wonderful feeling in the world knowing she sees me that way," I said honestly. The smile on B's face matched my own.

The next day while I was at work, apparently B had a very important grown up discussion with Hayley. When I came home they sat me down, and B asked me if I would be willing to adopt Hayley as my own. I couldn't have been happier. Soon Hayley was going to be Hayley Haywood, and I loved the sound of it. We were becoming a family, a real family that loved each other to no end. All that was left to do was pop the question. I know only four months, and some days had passed since we've been together but honestly, when you love someone as much as I loved my two girls, time didn't really matter.

We never discussed marriage, and I didn't know if it was something she wanted from me, especially since she was a divorced woman. Did she want to get on that boat again?

Well...if I didn't ask, I would never know!

So, I took Hayley to see her Nana, and planned an incredible night just for us. Since the new house, the therapy sessions with Hayley, the adoption papers, B planning her return to the University, and me working again full time; quality time to our selves was becoming rare.

I took her to the nicest restaurant in town; we ate, drank, and danced all evening. When we made it back home she fell against my chest when she saw the sight before her. I had my sister come while we were gone, and place Orchids as far as the eye could see on every surface that didn't have a candle on it. Said candles were lit, casting a romantic and serene glow across the entire room. Calla lily pedals, and sprigs of baby's-breath led a trail to the staircase, and up to our bathroom. The tub was currently full of scented bubbles as steam rose off of the water. The windows were open, the curtains blowing in the mid-September breeze inside.

The rest of the night was devoted to her and her only. I worshiped this woman like no other man ever would.

I settled between her legs, and kissed her mouth as the early morning sun streamed through the windows. I was gently calling her name, cupping her cheek as I ran my fingers through her hair. She grumbled under her breath, and slowly opened one eye.

"So I guess I'm not dreaming?" she asked, slowly opening the other eye.

"Not dreaming," I chuckled, kissing between her breasts.

"You do realize you're in trouble now, right?" she asked.

"And why is that?" I replied amused.

"Because you've gone, and spoiled me Haywood," she said, smiling, "Now, I never want to wake up any other way than this."

I quirked an eyebrow, and smiled deviously before tracing around her breast with my mouth, and I'm pretty sure she could tell what she always does to me at that moment, against her inner thigh.

"Okay, so maybe there are *some* other ways I'd like to be woken up too," she said with a moan. I continued my voyage upwards over her collarbone and across her neck before finding my resting spot behind her left ear.

"Anything you want Angel," I answered; she gripped the white sheets of our over sized bed, and closed her eyes.

Pulling away, I kissed across her cheek, and stopped right at her lips before leaning back, and looking into her eyes, they held nothing but all the love in the world for me, and I just stayed there, waiting for her to see it.

Finally she reached up with her left hand to caress my face.

"What are …" she started, *"Oh, my god,"* she breathed as her eyes widened before they were suddenly flooded with unshed tears. A few began to fall when she blinked, and I quickly swiped at them, but more fell anyway as her eyes traveled from nervous me, to the *stunning* sapphire, and diamonds engagement ring sitting on her ring finger.

"Col…how….when?" she stammered.

"B?" I called.

Oh, god. Why was she crying? Was it too soon to ask? Fuck! God dammit, I knew I should have waited!

I didn't think I read the signals wrong, but I supposed I couldn't have been all that sure. But I knew. I just *knew* B was feeling what I was on every level. A woman does not look at a man that way without wanting forever, and my Angel, her entrancing eyes were like no other. They pulled me in, made me forget every worry I've ever had, and have me only thinking about tomorrows. Tomorrows full of moments with her, with Hayley. I just knew she wanted this too. I felt the love pouring off of her yesterday and every damn day before that. Damn near drank that shit up last night at the restaurant, and almost proposed to her in the bathtub while she rode me as the overwhelming power of what we shared made my fucking heart stop.

I knew she wanted it….

Then why in hell was she still crying!

"Angel?" I called again. This time, she smiled a real smile, and then her smile done up, and turned teasing on my ass. Oh, no!

"Hypothetically speaking…" she sniffled, "What would you do if I said no?" she asked, trying unsuccessfully to hide her smile.

"You want the manly answer or the real answer?" I asked with my own smile, just happy she was at least speaking to me now.

"The real one," she answered.

Cry like a bitch, and beg her until I turned blue in the face.

"Try my hardest to persuade you to say yes," I said instead.

"You are so lying," she laughed, throwing her head back, "You know that was not what you were just thinking," she added. Not being able to fight it, I laughed with her before stopping her giggles with my lips. I cupped both side of her face in my hands, and just stared into those trouble making eyes of hers, before saying what my heart wanted me to say. What it needed to say.

"B, I need you more than I need air to breathe, and now is not the time to be calling me 'cheesy'," I added with a pointed look. She smiled, and lightly shook her head.

"B,ti amo così tanto che non posso nemmeno immaginarmi per un altro momento come sarebbe la mia vita senza di te in lei . Tu sei il mio cuore, la mia anima , il mio inizio e la mia sono mai stato più come me stesso che quando sono con te," **(B, I love you so damn much, and cannot even begin to think of another moment of what my life would be like without you in it. You are my heart, my soul, my beginning, and my end. I've never been more like myself than when I am with you.)** I wiped away a few of the new tears that fell from her eyes.

"Ho bisogno di te nella mia vita...completamente." I added. **(I need you in my life....completely.)** Her chin quivered, her eyes quickly closed, and her light sobs quieted, apparently waiting for the next words out of my mouth. I took a deep breath, and placed my hand over her heart, smiling when I felt it skip against my skin.

"Belladonna Rivers, vorresti sposarmi?" **(Belladonna Rivers, will you marry me?)** I whispered, not wanting to break the moment, and quietly praying that I didn't just ruin everything. When her small and trembling hand ran through my hair, I closed my eyes, and leaned into her touch. My eyes shot open, and trained on hers when her other hand caressed along my jaw, and across my bottom lip.

"Yes," she squeaked. I chuckled. She rolled her eyes before clearing her throat quietly.

"Yes, Collin," she answered in a voice so damn strong that it left no doubt that she meant every word.

"Oh mio Dio si! **(Oh my God yes!)** A freaking thousand times yes," she added while softly touching my face, staring at me with eyes that literally owned me, and always would.

"I love you," I chuckled. It was the only thing I could think of at the moment...still good nonetheless.

"I love you," she replied, still rubbing her nails across the hairs on the nape of my neck. Then she smiled again…Uh oh.

"Now show me," she challenged, writhing her hips against mine, I groaned, and she smiled, the same damn smile she gave me at the restaurant before she gave me a fucking foot job under the table at a goddamn five star restaurant. God I loved her.

"Come on, Haywood," she teased, dragging out my last name, "Don't you want to make love to your *fiancé* for the first time?" she asked pushing out her bottom lip in an adorable pout while lifting her hips, and making her heat hover over Mr. always-up-around-her. Right before she bit that damn bottom lip.

Okay, she wanted it. She was going to get it.

"Your wish, my command, Angel," I answered, right before I lifted my hips, and trusted into her, biting my tongue at how fucking *good* she felt, and feeling her already begin to quiver.

Sweet victory.

I watched in rapture as she buried her head against the pillow while her eyes snapped shut, and her mouth opened in a silent yell. I smiled when her nails gripped the sheets and the pillow when I tilted my hips, and trusted upwards right toward her spot. I almost did some fucking caveman chest pounding shit when her eyes rolled back as she screamed out at the top of her lungs. Wanting to be the best goddamn fiancé that I could be I happily obliged, and made love to her. I had her screaming, making her moan, and yelling out my name over, and over.

Right before she collapsed against my sweat-soaked, panting chest, all I could think about was *'happily ever after and shit'*, before laughing, and earning a puzzled look from my *fiancé*.

CHAPTER 28

How did he know? This was my ring, *the* ring. The double-band princess cut with a solitaire sapphire surrounded by small pave diamonds ring. *The* ring that I've dreamed about, the one that Mika and I…oh, wait! Mika of course, she helped him. I loved that little one so damn much right now. Just the thought that she was in on this…that she…shoot! There was no stopping the waterworks! I had to call her back. She called earlier but honestly having that man on top of me or under me or behind me or…well, you get the picture. I didn't bother answering. But hot damn I get to marry that tongue!

Okay, back on track, I had to remember Mika…caller ID…I had to call her back, but first how in hell was I supposed to stop this man. Screw it all if you even *think* that I had *any* mental, let alone, hormonal capability of stopping his hands as they slowly traveled up my inner thigh, right before his middle finger started…

"Oh god," I moaned.

Oh, for fuck's sake…excuse my language.

Okay…Right. I was supposed to do something, right?

"Mika!" I exclaimed happily, and a little shocked I remembered. Seeing as how that tongue attached to a man built to torment me stopped its licking, and stroking down my stomach. When a head full of brown-colored hair popped up, I'm pretty sure I said that out loud. The amused blue eyes, arched brow, and pursed lips officially sealed the deal.

"Now I've been called many things in my life," he began, but stopped, and started laughing when I narrowed my eyes at him before hitting him in the head with a pillow. It only made him laugh harder.

"It's your fault in the first place," I said, trying to pretend to be mad at him. As if that was even a possibility.

But it was his fault! Ever since the morning proposal, and what happened afterward …mmm…*ahem…I* have been trying to call my sister in law back to tell her, and to thank her for everything she did. Also, if I was being honest I wanted to save Riley's sanity. Lord only knew what she was putting him through at that moment. It was already after twelve in the afternoon, and I hadn't come around to calling her back yet. She was small, but she was a fierce little fairy whose bad side you did *not* want to be on. Just trust me on that.

So anyway, as I was saying, I had been trying (not very hard mind you) to distract Collin enough in order to be able to use the phone. Sounds simple right? Ha! Simple my butt! He got one glimpse of the engagement ring on my hand as it rested on his lower stomach, and it was like, *hello!* Who would have thought wearing his ring would make him want me more? More than he already did? Who thought that was even possible! I sure didn't. Sexual, primitive, possessive ….Don't think I was complaining though.

"And exactly how is it my fault?" he asked…right before he pulled the already taut, sensitive skin of my breast into his mouth.

"Evil bastard," I whispered, clutching onto his hair, and holding his head exactly where the hell it was. I felt his smile spread across the skin of my breast before his chest softly vibrated with laughter, and at that exact moment all I wanted to do was slap him!

"That's it Mr. Magic Member….move!" I said while pushing his head off of me. That wasn't needed. The moment my verbal diarrhea left my mouth his head shot up, his eyes met mine, and I've never seen him try to hold back a laugh more than he did at that moment. Poor thing was actually turning a little red.

"Mr. Magic Member?" he squeezed out before quickly shutting his lips. Oh, those lips….

"What?" I shrugged. He was still silent. Lips squeezed shut. Eyes gleaming full of amusement. "It works wonders, and you know it Collin," I said, dead serious.

And that broke the dam. Collin laughed so hard he fell back onto the bed shaking it now for an entirely different reason. He was also saying 'oh god, B' for an entirely different reason too, but that wasn't important.

Oh, who in hell was I kidding? The smile on my face damn near hurt when it spread at the sound of his laughter. Smiling, I just sat up on my elbows, and stared. He was glorious. That was the only conceivable word able to come close to what I saw before my eyes. Now you shouldn't get me wrong, the brooding, cocky Collin was sexy as hell. Though the one lying next to me; laughing, and smiling with his eyes shut, mouth open, hands lying on his bare chest, the one who lets his guard down, and shows you the *real* him. A man that would do anything for the people he loved, a man that was devoting his life to raise a little girl that wasn't his, and a man that made me happy beyond belief. Well *that* one just makes you fall in love with him all over again.

I dove for my phone on the side table since I *finally* had him distracted enough to have the chance to call Mika. Unfortunately, the moment I pressed the call button his head popped up off of the bed, he grabbed me by my waist, and pulled me on top of him. I squealed, but before he could speak I grabbed the pillow I launched at him earlier, and laid it over his face hearing him laugh again just as Mika picked up.

"B," she squealed. Good lord, I could actually see her clapping. Time to have some fun…

"Hi Mika what's up, you called?" I asked. The silence that followed could only suggest she was just staring at the phone with her 'what the hell' face on. Collin just shook his head…still under the pillow.

"What's…? But don't you have something to….?" she asked, breaking off at the end. Oh, that was so good!

"Something to what Mika? I just called to say hi, and to apologize for calling you back a little late. We were so busy, I just lost track of the time," I said, feeling Mr. Chuckles start to laugh again. I leaned over, and licked his nipple. He groaned. That ought to do it.

"But…didn't Collin? I mean…wasn't he going to…" she started.

Suddenly she took in a deep breath, and let it out long, and slow. Uh oh, "Where's Collin?" she demanded, dangerously low.

Gulp!

"He's here. Why Mika? Is there something wrong?" I was so going to hell in a hand basket.

"That's unknown at the moment," she answered through what could only have been gritted teeth. "Now where is he?" she asked again.

Warning! Pissed off Pixie in 'T minus 10!'

"Here he is. Hold on," I said, trying not to laugh I pressed 'speaker' on the phone, and removed the pillow from Collin's face.

Big freaking *uh oh*.

The moment the pillow was gone I was met with blazing blue eyes, and he slowly shook his head from side to side before mouthing 'payback'. I should have taken that as a warning. Some part of me was trying to beat that thought into my skull. But all I noticed was the mouth. The sudden smirk on the damn thing once its owner realized what I was staring at had me leaning over for a kiss.

"Ahem!" God darn it! Wait until I get out of here and…

"Hi Mimi, my favorite little sister in the whole wide world," the lips with the velvet voice answered. Once again I was enthralled, staring at the man like the apparent wanton horn dog I was, and once again completely his fault.

"Don't *hi* me, Collin Haywood! What the hell? When you came to me, and asked for help…when I showed you B's choice of the ri…" she yelled.

"You're on speaker Mika," Collin interrupted. She gasped, and I squeezed my lips shut to keep silent.

"You are so evil," he whispered in my ear. I might have taken offense had he not laughed right afterward.

"But I…you said that….but B and….enga….you….AH!" she stammered before yelling out in a huff. Did she hit something?

"Ow! Shit, Mika baby," Riley yelled out from farther away.

"Oh, my God, I'm so sorry Riley!" she answered. Collin and I were goners. I dropped the phone onto the bed next to us, buried my face in his neck, and laughed my butt off while Collin whooped it up before saying 'poor Riley'.

"I think we should tell her before someone else gets hurt," he said after calming down.

"Yeah, namely us," I answered, trying to stifle my giggles as I called her name.

"Mimi?"

"What!" she snapped. Okay, so I guessed we may get hurt either way. Collin's slight cringe let me know he was thinking the same thing.

"He asked me," I answered, taking a deep breath before looking into suddenly calm eyes. Even the lips couldn't compete with those at that moment.

She was still silent.

"Mimi…"

"Say what now?" she interrupted, my smile widened. We got her; na, na, na, na, na, naaa.

"We're engaged, honey," I answered, smiling at Collin.

"You…you're…" she stammered.

"I asked her this morning," Collin answered softly, looking directly in my eyes, "I put the ring on her finger after she fell asleep last night, and asked her as soon as she woke up a little over four hours ago," he completed. Collin's finger came up, and slowly stroked my cheek.

"She squeaked 'yes'," he added, smiling.

I closed my eyes, and leaned my forehead against his, loving the feeling of his arms tightening around me. My heart began beating rapidly against his chest, as his did the same against mine.

"I love you," I said against his lips.

"I…" Was as far as he got to replying, because we suddenly heard the panicky voice of Riley over the phone.

"Mika? Baby are you okay? Mika answer me!" Riley said frantically. What the?

"Mika? Is she…?" I started, but was quickly cut off when the *loudest,* and possibly the most excitable squeal my ears have ever experienced pierced through the phone.

"Son of a bitch," Collin said, taking the phone, and shoving it under the pillow. If only that helped, it barely muffled Mika's cry of glee, and Riley's cries of 'oh, shut up!' Poor man was going to need a hearing aid after that.

"B? B!" Mika's muffled yell called. Shaking my head, I removed the phone from under the pillow.

"Are you through being supersonic now?" Collin asked.

"Oh, shut up!" she demanded, "How could you? How *could* you B? Put me through that, and making me think he didn't ask!" she ranted. "And *you*, you fool! I was going to kill you Collin, brother or not. I was going to send your ass six feet under, then run, and hide from B's wrath until she calmed down enough to let me explain. Once I did explain what you said you'd do, and then didn't do, she'd probably bring your ass back to life just to kill you again herself!" she added. Collin arched his brow at me in question. I just shrugged, and nodded. He rolled his eyes.

After her ranting, which lasted another dreadful eleven minutes, she asked about the proposal. Collin said it word for word. I almost became the boohoo chick from that morning again. Luckily, Riley's interrupting congratulations nipped that right in the bud, and he said he couldn't wait to see us.

I was literally the happiest woman on earth, and I couldn't wait to start living my happily ever after.

CHAPTER 29

During the next few weeks B and I filed for our marriage license. My mother and sister turned into rabid wedding planners, and unfortunately my angel had been sick for a few weeks now. I have been pestering her to go to the doctor's office today. Hayley was with my mother, having the house to my self I wanted to surprise my wife to be, and daughter (I still grin at the thought) with a little surprise I had to pick up. A week a go I saw an announcement in the newspaper for Shepherd puppies being sold, and I called right away. Hayley loved Sophie, my mother's Shepherd, so much I decided she should have one of her own. I hadn't spoken to B about it, but I knew she would be okay with this. She had mentioned before the fact that she never had a dog, and always wanted one. I was suppose to pick him or her up today, but of course as faith would have it work called, and here I was, immersed in a case up to my fucking neck.

Some people just didn't understand the concept of a fucking Saturday. Déjà vu someone? Was it written on my forehead that I liked working on Saturdays? Okay, maybe I was not *at* work, but still making me work *from* home is almost as cruel. I was on the phone with my partner; Jonas was nice guy, one of the elders as they call them. He's been with the bureau for almost forty years, and works by the book like no one else, so it was sometimes hard to do things like I usually did…you know throw the book out the fucking window, and go with my instincts!

"The 'Meredith Johnson case'. She disappeared from her house last Saturday night, and never came back. She was 26, brunette, brown eyes –a pretty woman. Her family is desperate. She's the sixth one this month, and she's from New Jersey like the last girl who disappeared, Angela Casten."

He faxed me a picture of Meredith. His description was precise: brunette, brown eyes, and beautiful features, a pretty woman.

"So do you think it's the same Kidnapper?" I asked. My question came immediately.

"Yes, we suspect he's the same man. But we didn't find any footprints in her flat. Only her bedroom seemed disturbed so I concluded he probably did the kidnapping during her sleep or at least at night, she must have fought with him."

"No broken windows, no bullets?" I asked.

"No trace. Just the same note we found the last time…"

He sighed, and I reached for my file with other details about the case. The same shit as last week! Angela Casten was missing without a trace, the same as Victoria Mead, and the rest of the women.

The kidnapper had his own style: he was taking the victims without leaving any footprints, but in change he was leaving a note on a red sheet of paper *'Don't worry, she's safe'*. Of course the kidnapper was probably suffering from a psychological problem; B thinks maybe an obsessive compulsive disorder. I wasn't really supposed to share this kind of information with her, but I trusted her with my life. As a psychologist who has worked in a penitentiary with criminals of all kind, she has been a great help to me, and this case. Of course, the less detail's I shared with her the better. So I only told her what she would need to know in order to give me some kind of helpful information on our suspect. The case was getting more and more difficult because we couldn't find any fucking trace of the missing women. The note was the only evidence we had. But we did notice something; all missing women were redheads, and brunettes.

"I'm going in my office to study the file. I'll talk to you later Collin; call me if you figure out anything alright?" Jonas said.

"Sure thing, it's not like I have *anything* else to do on a Saturday you know?" I said sarcastically. Jonas knew how much I hated working weekends, I have a family, and I don't live a hermit life like he does.

Jonas was about fifty-ish, but he actually looked more like sixty five.

His hair was white all over, although lucky for him he still had them all. He wasn't very tall, and his beer gut was pretty evident, it didn't take away his talent though. He was one of the best, and I was damn proud to have him as a partner. It could be hard sometimes to deal with him when he got into one of his broody moods. Davidson, a colleague from work, told me Jonas lost his wife to cancer three years ago. They never had any children, and most of his family was dead. The ones still alive he didn't want to speak to them.

He chuckled, "I know…I know…sorry. If it makes you feel better let's close this god damn case quickly so we can get on with our lives." he laughed again.

"Yeah, alright…I'll talk to you later," I hung up, and checked the time…again.

Her appointment should have been over half, and hour ago…why hasn't she called me yet? Hoping she was alright, and trying not to overreact or panic I tried to concentrate on my work. Since the daycare incident, I had a hard time when they were away from me. I came too close for comfort to losing both of them, and it scared the shit out of me when I wasn't close to my girls. I tried to keep the worry to myself, because I knew it was only a tad bit of paranoia. Sometimes I could deal with it no problem, better than other times when I felt so anxious I couldn't breathe until they returned.

Nearly two hours later, I was really starting to panic when I heard my favorite sound in the world.

"We're home!" I jumped out of my chair, and was in the hallway within seconds scooping up my little girl into my arms.

CHAPTER 30

Collin's worried expression, and continuous nagging was the only reason I was sitting here in this examining room allowing my doctor to stick needles in my veins. The things I would do for that man.

"Could just be stress. Your life is a little crazy right now B," Dr. Pacheco patted my hand affectionately. She'd been our doctor, Hayley and I, ever since we moved to the big apple.

"But it's a good crazy," I mumbled as she removed the needle from my arm.

"Good or not, any lifestyle change can affect your digestive system. The blood tests may provide some answers," Dr. Pacheco looked down at her chart, "Everything else looks good. Since you're getting married soon, will you need contraception?"

"Yes, no, maybe?" I replied with a confused smile, "We haven't really talked about it."

She chuckled, "Well, let me give you a prescription just in case…better safe than sorry!"

"You could say that," I smiled happily.

"Good, well good luck with that. Are your cycles regular?" my smile faded.

"I guess so?" I said. *What is today's date?* I thought.

Dr. Pacheco raised an eyebrow, "You guess so?"

What the hell was today's date? I thought again.

I blinked rapidly, and gasped. I could literally see the light bulb illuminate over Dr. Pacheco's dark brown head. Of course, I may have just been hallucinating. The dull white of the walls and the sterile smell of the place may have had an effect on my brain.

"B?" Dr. Pacheco's voice was soft, "Is it possible that this isn't the flu at all?" she asked, and I said nothing.

"You didn't mention any other symptoms," she commented as she scanned my chart. "Of course; the blood tests will show…" her voice dimmed, I couldn't hear her anymore my heartbeat was thundering so loudly in my ears.

"B, you look pale. Do you need to lie down?" she asked me, and I finally vocalized my internal question.

"Dr. Pacheco, what is today's date?" I demanded.

"Today is the third of November." she said.

It was a new month? I counted on my fingers. Once. Twice. Again. Dr. Pacheco immediately started shouting out symptoms.

"Morning sickness?"

I shook my head, "Only nauseous a few times in the past few weeks"

"Fatigue?"

"Yes, but I'm planning a wedding, and we just settled into our new house…" I answered.

She nodded, "Emotional?"

"I've been crying over the dumbest things," I whispered softly. During yesterday's fitting, Mika, and Claire had shown me a beautiful tiara she thought would look perfect with my dress. When I tried it on, and looked at myself in the mirror, I immediately dissolved into tears. Scared the crap out of them too!

"When was your last period?" she asked softly. I closed my eyes.

"I honestly can't remember," I admitted.

She patted my hand again. I looked down at her hands, they were a soft brown, and she had beautiful nails. I didn't know what ethnicity she was, Spanish maybe? But she was a very pretty woman. Her dark eyes were comforting, and the accent in her voice was always very soothing to me.

"Well, we'll know in a few minutes. The blood test shouldn't take long," she reassured me. I took long cleansing breaths as she sat by my side, continually patting my hand.

"B, would it really be so terrible?" she asked gently.

"No," I smiled as I wiped away a tear. Again with the crying! "It would be wonderful, though a little out of order," I shrugged helplessly. Moments later, the nurse walked back into the room. I watched Dr. Pacheco's face as she scanned the results. She thanked the nurse as she walked out the door. She then turned toward me with a sweet smile on her face. I was not going to hurl. I was not going to hurl.

"Well honey, you won't need that contraception after all," she grinned.

I picked up Hayley from Claire's, and had the hardest time not blurring out 'I'm pregnant' at any given moment. So I scooted out of there as fast as politeness permitted. Hayley was sitting in the middle of the largest sandbox in the park. There were a couple of children playing along with her, and I watched with contentment as the trio shared buckets and shovels while they painstakingly developed their castles in the sand. They worked diligently….cooperatively….each person shaping his dirt in precise detail so that the three formations would join, and create a masterpiece.

"The best thing about the sandbox…" Hayley's friend said, "…..is that we aren't on the beach, so the ocean waves won't ruin it," she said. I didn't know her name, but she was very pretty. Her red curls fell around her shoulders, her big blue eyes were wide, and I just loved her little patch of freckles on her nose. The other kid with them was an older boy with black hair, and dark eyes.

I glanced up at the darkening sky. The clouds were beginning to roll in. I looked back down at the sand box, and noticed Hayley looking up at the clouds as well.

"It's going to wain," Hayley replied matter-of-factly, and pride swelled in my heart. My little girl was so smart.

How would she react to the news? Slowly, my hand ghosted along my stomach. Of course, there was nothing to feel. No protruding tummy just yet, but that didn't keep me from gingerly running my fingers along my skin. I didn't need physical, tangible proof. I could feel *her* in my heart. I could feel *him* in my veins. Boy or girl, it didn't matter at all. Was Collin going to have a preference? Will Hayley? And how was I going to tell them?

I was a little nervous about telling Collin I was pregnant. It was easy to predict his reaction, but I still had doubts. Hayley was a bit trickier. Would she feel threatened? She's had me all to herself for so long. Would she be willing to share her mother? Would she be willing to share Collin...her father?

In a moment of fear, I had dialed Dr. Annie's number. She had encouraged me to include Hayley as much as possible with every aspect of including a new baby into our routine. She suggested that she help decorate the nursery, choose toys for the baby, and pick the stuffed animals. I thanked her, and then felt guilty. Dr. Annie was the first person I'd told I was pregnant.

But I knew Collin would forgive me. This was important, and I needed to know how to proceed. Also, I had an idea, and I wanted the therapist's approval before involving Hayley. To my immense relief, and happiness, she had approved. A soft echo of thunder rumbled in the distance, prompting the other parents to grab their children, and pull them out of the park. Hayley said goodbye to her new friends, and my heart broke a little when her beautiful face fell as she examined their unfinished sand castle.

"It's not even waining yet," Hayley grumbled as she filled her bucket with dirt. After a few moments she carefully tipped it over, and pulled it away revealing a perfect castle tower.

"Let me help," I offered as I slowly climbed into the sand box. Hayley's face brightened as she handed me a bucket. I dutifully shoveled dirt into the blue pail.

"It needs a towew hewe," she explained.

"And which side is that?" I prompted, and Hayley grinned. Collin had been working on this for a few days with her.

"Left," she said.

"Good job," I smiled. We quietly went back to work. The thunder was still rumbling in the distance, so we worked quickly. It took us another half hour, but finally the towers were formed, and our sand castle was complete. We smiled at each other, and Hayley scampered into my lap as we sat back, admiring our work.

"I have a secret to tell you," I whispered, and watched her face light up with excitement. If there was one thing that thrilled her, it was keeping a secret.

"A secwet from who?" she asked.

"Well, from everyone right now," I replied thoughtfully, "But we should probably tell daddy tonight."

"Is it good?"

"I think it's a great one," I ventured carefully, "But I wanted to tell you, and then you could help me tell daddy."

"Okay," Hayley agreed. I took a deep breath, and turned her around in my lap so she could face me. Her tiny hands ghosted along my teary cheek.

"Are you cwying again?" she asked annoyingly. It bothered me that she'd noticed I'd been crying so much lately. I had just been so emotional, and I'd been unable to hide it.

"Yes, because I'm happy," I told her.

"You must be *weally* happy. You cwy *all* the time," she said, exaggerating the last words. I laughed. I was happy…deliriously happy.

"That's part of the secret. There's a reason I'm so happy," I said, and Hayley stared at me expectantly. I took another deep breath as I gazed down into the mirror image of my own green eyes.

"I'm happy because of the wedding…and our new house….and because you want to call Collin daddy."

"I love daddy, so it's okay I call him that?" she asked gently. My heart constricted in my chest, "Yes, baby."

"I'm not a baby," Hayley scrunched her nose, "Babies awe little, and poop in a diapew…." she said scrunching up her nose, and there was my opening.

"You're right," I agreed, "You're not a baby. You're such a big girl. But….what do you think about babies? Do you think you'd like a baby brother or sister?"

She grew thoughtful putting her index finger against her small lips and looking up at the sky she said, "I don't know, babies cwy *a lot.*"

I couldn't help but laugh again. "Sometimes, but only when they're little, they mostly just sleep all the time," I said, and she remained quiet as she contemplated this new information. I began to get a little nervous. Was I doing this right?

"Awe *we* getting a baby?" Hayley finally asked. The question startled me. How had she made that connection?

"Would that be okay?" I asked hesitantly.

"I think so," she replied thoughtfully, "Would it be a boy or a giwl?"

"I don't know," I answered honestly, relief flowing through my body. She didn't seem too upset at the idea.

Suddenly, her eyes flashed with excitement. "Can we pick?"

I laughed, "No, we don't get to pick."

"Who gets to pick?"

Dr. Annie had told me Hayley was an inquisitive child, and would probably ask a lot of questions. She also suggested that I keep my explanations vague until I was actually showing some kind of bump. It would be hard to explain to Hayley that a baby was growing inside of me. But if she could actually touch my growing tummy, it would give her a better understanding of what was going on.

"We'll let daddy explain who picks," I replied sweetly. It seemed only fair, I was doing the hard stuff here...

"Does daddy know we'we getting a baby?" Hayley asked excitedly.

"Not yet. *That's* the secret," I noted Hayley was using the phrase 'getting a baby' as if we were just going to store, and picking one out. She had absolutely no frame of reference, so I was content with letting her visualize the situation that way, at least for now.

"Will you help me tell him?" Hayley nodded excitedly, and I hugged her close.

"We're home!" I announced as we made our way through the living room.

"Remember," I whispered down to Hayley. I placed my finger over my lips; she nodded, and giggled excitedly.

"Finally," Collin exclaimed appearing from the hallway leading to his study. His face was etched with relief as he pulled Hayley into his arms. "I expected to hear from you after your appointment."

"I'm sorry," I murmured as he softly kissed my cheek, and led us to the couch.

"We went to the pawk," Hayley announced happily as she snuggled into her father's lap, "Mommy helped me build the *best* sand castle evew..... Can we tell him now?"

Dr. Annie also reminded me Hayley was four years old. This secret couldn't stay a secret for long.

"Yes," I whispered softly before turning my attention to Collin, "We have something for you," I said, and motioned to Hayley. He watched as she leapt out of his arms, and raced to her small white and pink Cinderella bag. She quickly opened it, and pulled the little wrapped box out. Hayley rushed back to her place on the sofa, and snuggled into her father's lap again.

"What's this?" Collin wondered, and he shook the box. It made a slight rattling noise, which was actually pretty perfect considering what was wrapped inside.

Hayley giggled, "Mommy let me pick the wowds."

"The words?" Collin smiled softly at me, kissed Hayley's forehead, and brushed the tears away from my cheeks. Freaking hormones!

"Huwwy Daddy," Hayley groaned as he tugged on the gift wrap.

"Okay, okay," Collin laughed as he carefully un-wrapped the package. I took a deep breath, but I found I didn't really need it. Telling the man you loved...the man you were marrying... you were pregnant with his child should have been the most nerve-wracking moment of your life. A complete surprise, although it probably shouldn't be considering we'd done nothing to prevent it but still...this would be a complete surprise to him, and to his family. Shouldn't I be a little concerned? Shouldn't I be nervous? But I didn't feel any of those things. All I felt was peace and a sense of completion as if the puzzle pieces were all there, and the picture was *almost* complete.

Sometimes the most perfect and most beautiful things in life are effortless. My father's words washed over me while I watched Collin's astonished face as he lifted the tiny silver rattle from the confines of the gift box. I had prepared myself for this moment, trying to decide on the perfect words. How did you tell the man you loved you were carrying his child?

"We'we getting a baby!" Hayley's happy voice echoed around the empty room. That's how you do it.

Collin's bright blue eyes glanced at Hayley… then back to the rattle… and then his penetrating gaze settled on my face.

"We're…" Collin's voice was just a whisper, "…a baby?"

"Read the inscription," I whispered tearfully. His glowing eyes flashed to the rattle, and looked closely at the engraving.

My big sister loves me.
~Baby Haywood~
2011

"We'we getting a baby!" Hayley squealed again.

"Hayley, honey, can you go to your room please? I'd like to talk with daddy alone," I murmured as Collin's eyes remained transfixed on the rattle in his hand. She jumped out of Collin's lap, and raced toward her room. The room was suddenly too quiet, and I fidgeted nervously as Collin continued staring at the rattle.

"Say something," I begged softly. Wasn't he happy? Collin blinked rapidly, and turned his head toward me.

"We're *getting* a baby?" he said.

"We're *having* a baby," I clarified, "This wasn't something I could explain to our daughter, but she understood *getting* a baby…so….."

"*Our* daughter….." Collin whispered softly, and smiled.

"She's calling you daddy isn't she?" I said smiling back at him.

"Yeah, she is, and you don't have the flu?" he asked. I shook my head.

"We're really having a baby?" his voice was incredulous.

"Yes," I replied meekly, "Dr. Pacheco thinks July…" I trailed off. The expression on Collin's face was unlike anything I'd ever seen. This wasn't the reaction I'd been expecting at all. Wasn't he happy? I would literally die right here in this spot if he was anything short of ecstatic.

I watched as Collin placed a soft kiss against the inscription on the rattle before gently placing it back in its box. He carefully placed the box on the oak coffee table, and lowered himself to the floor. He was kneeling before me, his eyes gazing reverently into my face. With the softest of touches, Collin brushed each side of my face with his fingertips.

"Words cannot describe how much I love you," he murmured adoringly, "This morning; I woke up before the alarm, and just watched you sleep. I have memorized every curve of your face….the flutter of your eyelashes…. the way you breathe when you're sleeping."

His hands trailed down my body, finally resting on my stomach. Gently, he lifted the hem of my shirt, and I sighed as his fingers brushed across my skin.

"And as I was staring at you, I actually thought to myself there was no way in hell I could possibly love you more than I did right in that moment… but now….." he leaned closer, and pulled my shirt higher. I gasped as he lowered his head, and placed sweet, worshipful kisses along my stomach. I leaned back against the couch, and he followed my movement by leaning forward, still kissing my stomach.

"You've given me everything I've ever wanted, B. Mi hai proprio cuore e l'anima e adesso so che io non ti amo abbastanza. Ogni singolo giorno, io sono caduto un po 'più innamorato di te e so che questo è come sarà per il resto della mia vita," **(You own me, heart, and soul., and I know now that I'll never love you enough. Every single day, I've fallen a little more in love with you, and I know this is how it's going to be for the rest of my life.)**

The tears streamed down my cheeks, and Collin gently lifted his hand, wiping them away.

"We're having a baby," he whispered softly, and I noticed a tear trickle down his cheek, as well. I sniffled, and placed my fingertip along his face.

"Everything has happened so fast," I murmured gently. I cupped his face in my hands, and he melted into my touch, "It's so hard to keep up…. so hard to process it all…."

"I know," Collin whispered, taking one of my hands away from his face, and placing a soft kiss against my wrist, "But honestly, when you remove all of the drama, it's actually pretty easy. I love you. You love me. We have a beautiful daughter, a baby on the way, and we're getting married. I was even going to get us a puppy today."

I giggled, "You were going to get a puppy? Really?! You make everything sound so simple," I smiled happily. He chuckled, and kissed my hand again.

"It *is* simple," Collin assured me, "Look at what we have now...."

"It was all worth it," I whispered softly, and I knew it was true. My misery with Brian....his loss of Sarah...Hayley's kidnapping...both of us getting fired, but every ounce of heartbreak had brought us here. It was worth every minute.

"I can't wait to be your wife," I murmured, and the smile reflected on his face made my heart soar.

"I can't wait to be your husband," Collin sighed softly, and he leaned down once again to place a soft kiss on my exposed stomach.

"And I can't wait to be your daddy," he whispered.

CHAPTER 31

We were having a boy...I was over the moon happy. I was so happy I went crazy for the following weeks...hell the following months too. I took Hayley with me, and we chose every single piece of furniture for her new little brother. Everything she picked was natural wood, the crib sheet set was Winnie the Pooh. She wanted trucks, and cars everywhere, so I got everything related to trucks, and cars like she asked.

My mother cried for hours when we told...well when we let Hayley tell my parents. Hayley wanted to say the secret to everyone herself. Who was I to deny this to my little girl? Who was I to deny anything to both of them? B and I discussed the puppy surprise I wanted to do, and she made me see reason that it wasn't a good idea at the moment. With me working full time, her taking care of our baby boy and Hayley, time for a puppy would be limited. Of course, I agreed. Whatever she wanted was fine with me. Though, I have to admit I was a little disappointed. She also decided to postpone going back to school until the baby was old enough for day care. She couldn't start while she was pregnant, quit some months later to stay home, and start again the next year. She wanted her whole focus and energy on this new path she was choosing.

Anyway, back to the main topic: as soon as the rest of the family found out it was a boy, a war of testosterone erupted.

"I'll teach him football, GO PACKERS!" Riley shouted, as the godfather he was taking his role *very* seriously. My sister was beyond happy to be the godmother but a little sad our boy was probably not going to enjoy shopping as much as her, his sissy, his Nana, and mommy.

"No…no…no…sorry dude, hockey…he's gonna play hockey!" I argued.

"Well I'm not getting up at five in the morning for practice if *you* want him to play!" B said in my direction. We were all gathered at my parents for dinner, and I was keeping a close eye on my beautiful wife. Yes…wife. We got married as soon as she found out she was pregnant. My mother and sister were devastated since we decided on a quick and simple wedding. B didn't want to wait after she had the baby, and didn't want to get married looking like a cow, as she so delicately put it.

I kept telling her how absolutely gorgeous she was every chance I got, but she still thought she looked like an overgrown Beluga. Unfortunately, she hasn't been feeling too well for the past few days. She had been complaining about shortness of breath, and headaches. We went to see Dr. Pacheco, but she assured us everything was normal after she did a few tests. So, I've been watching her like a hawk.

"Well I think he'll play baseball. I was the best back in the day!" my dad added to the debate.

"You know what, *enough*…if luck is on our side he'll wear a tutu, and play in the Nut Cracker…so there…" B handed a dollar to Hayley who was giggling like there was no tomorrow, "Shut the fuck up about it!"

We were all stunned into silence.

Hormones…I tell you, it's some scary shit!

The evening went on perfectly, everyone was having fun, but I noticed my Angel looking paler, and paler. I went to see her sitting quietly in the corner of the living room looking out one of the windows that showed the backyard.

"Angel, are you okay?" I asked, and knelt next to her.

"I don't know Collin…something's wrong. I feel even worse than I did this morning." She did look worst, so I took matters into my own hands.

"Come on let's go see the doctor," I helped her up, and told the rest of the family where we were going.

Mika looked at us with worry in her eyes, "I'll stay here with Hayley, and we'll meet you there?"

I nodded, and all of them agreed to meet us at the hospital. We kissed Hayley goodbye, reassuring her we would see her in a little while.

As I settle B in the passenger seat of my truck, I couldn't help notice how her breath was shallower than before, and if possible her skin was paler, almost gray. I stepped on it, but still driving carefully to get to the hospital as fast as I could. When we got there I fetched a wheel chair, and brought her in, not really caring if I left the truck at the main entrance. They could tow it for all I fucking cared.

One nurse saw us, and came to me in a hurry wanting to know what was going on, and asked who our doctor was.

"Dr. Pacheco and we don't know…she's having trouble breathing and she's getting paler by the minute," I said.

B added, "I'm nauseous…and I've been stuck with a head ache since this morning." She sounded so weak; it was scaring the shit out of me. The nurse paged Dr. Pacheco, and they settled B in a private room. It didn't take long for the family to show up, but they were instructed to stay in the waiting area except for Hayley, she was with us.

"Mommy awe you okay? Is Josh okay?" she asked. Hayley chose her little brother's name like almost everything else, with our approval of course. We all agreed that Josh Haywood sounded perfect.

"I'll be fine princess, and so will Josh. Mommy's just feeling a little sick," she tried to convince her, but there was something in her eyes that told me she, herself, wasn't so sure.

Dr Pacheco arrived within the next fifteen minutes, and asked us to go wait outside while she did tests, and took blood from my wife. I was scared…scared to loose my son…scared of not knowing what was going on with my wife, my angel.

The doctor came back almost half an hour later.

"We're going into surgery for a c-section; we need to get the baby out as soon as possible," she said, and I made a motion to get up, but she lifted her hand to stop me. "I'm sorry Mr. Haywood, normally you would be allowed in the operating room with her, but in this case we can't let you. If you would like to speak with your wife before hand, now is the time."

With that said she turned around, and headed in the opposite direction.

What the fuck was going on? Why wouldn't they tell me anything?

I stood up. "Hayley princess, do you want to see mommy before Josh is born?" I asked her. She nodded, and took my hand. Nothing could have prepared me for the sight that greeted me. B's eyes were blood shot, and swollen, she kept fidgeting with her fingers. When she saw us she held out her arms for Hayley, and I placed her on the bed in the crook of her arm careful not to disturb the I.V.'s while I stood leaning against the wall next to her bed. I was at a loss for words seeing my strong, beautiful Angel so weak, and fragile.

"Hi honey," she said to Hayley.

"Hi mommy…Josh is coming?" she said in a small voice. B chuckled without emotion.

"Yes he is. Can you promise me something?"

Hayley nodded, and B answered her in a soft whisper. I don't know if I was supposed to hear but I did, and shivers ran down my spine.

"Be nice to your little brother okay? Share you're toys, and don't tease him too much," she asked, and Hayley promised to her mother she would try to be nice as long as he didn't touch her dolls.

"Good, now go see aunt Mika, and I'll see you soon…" she hugged her tight, "…I love you princess."

"Love you too mommy," she crawled down, and I watched from the door as she walked straight to the waiting area a few meters down the hall. When I came back to her side, B was staring out the window.

"How are you feeling, Angel?" I asked.

"Fine, the medication is helping. Are you ok? How are Hayley and everybody else holding up?"

"I'm fine, Hayley is just as strong as you are, and everyone else is fine." I sat next to her, and held her hands. When her eyes found mine, my heart squeezed. They were so sad, and empty. The glint in her beautiful green eyes was gone. When she spoke next, even though her voice was weak, I could feel how much love she had for us.

"Don't worry Collin…you'll all be fine."

"Angel, you'll be alright. Stop worrying, you'll get better, and we'll go home with our baby boy, Hayley, and you can go back to annoying the shit out of Mika," I said with a shaky voice. She chuckled.

"Collin, please let me say this…" she took a deep breath, and closed her eyes for a few seconds before going on, "You are the best husband I could have hoped for…the best friend, the best father. I seriously could not imagine being with anyone else but you. I'm not leaving you; I'm not ever leaving you. I'm always in your heart, and I love you more than words can describe." she whispered weakly.

"I love you too B, so much…don't worry about a thing, we'll all be here when you get out of the surgery." I was scared. I didn't like hearing her speak this way, but I figured she was probably just as scared as I was, and god knows the thoughts that go on in our heads when we're scared.

I told her one last time how much I loved her, kissed her stomach and kissed her lips tenderly before the nurses came in to wheel her bed into the surgery area to prep her. I went back to the waiting room, sat down with Hayley in my lap, and waited…

And waited…

And waited…

I must have fallen asleep, because a hand suddenly shook my shoulder gently.

"Collin honey, the doctor is coming over," my mother said. I opened my eyes, and saw Dr. Pacheco walking toward us. I looked at my watch; we've been waiting for nearly three hours.

What the hell took them so god damn long?

Mika took a sleeping Hayley from me, and I stood up meeting the doctor a few feet away.

"Hey doc… How's Josh? Is she back in her room? What happened?" I asked impatiently. The words kept flowing out of my mouth but when I saw her expression, all thoughts left me.

What…happened?

"Josh is fine, a little premature at 34 weeks, but all in all he's doing very well. We'll have to keep him for a few days to make sure all his vitals are working properly though. Once we know everything is fine then you can take him home, and we'll schedule weekly appointments to see his progress."

"That's wonderful doc, thank you," we all said, almost in unison.

"Can I see my wife now?" I asked. Dr. Pacheco looked at all of our faces, and spoke the words that shattered my world...

"I'm sorry Mr. Haywood...she...didn't make it," she said slowly.

The scream that followed ran through my ears like a noise in the background you can't quite figure out where it came from...Until I realized, as my mother was holding my hand, I was the one who was screaming. I fell to my knees, and my family gathered around me.

"I am so sorry, to all of you," Dr. Pacheco said. Mika was trying to hold back the sobs that were racking her body as she held Hayley, who miraculously hadn't woken up. "What...why...but she was..."

She took the words right out of my mouth as I stood again with the help of my father, and he sat me down in a nearby chair. I held my head in my hands as I tried to control the pain ripping my insides open. My head was throbbing, my hands were shaking, and all I could think about was waking up from this nightmare to see her beautiful sleeping face next to me.

"She had what we call Amniotic fluid embolism, it's a rare obstetric emergency where the amniotic fluid, fetal cells, hair, and other debris enters the blood stream via the placental bed of the uterus, and triggers an allergic reaction. This reaction then resulted in cardio respiratory collapse, and coagulopathy," she paused, took a deep breath, and continued. I tried to listen but only heard bits, and pieces. I couldn't concentrate through the pain in my chest, and fog in my head.

"That was the reason for her acute shortness of breath, hypotension, and headaches. Unfortunately during the delivery it rapidly progressed to a cardiac arrest before she lapsed into a coma, and her cardiovascular system collapsed," she explained.

I was in such pain, it all turned into a seething rage.

"How could you not prevent it? Do you realize what you have taken from me?" I said through clenched teeth. She cut me off before I could get even more fucking pissed off, and scream at her some more.

"Mr. Haywood this is a one in 20,000 case. The chance of this happening was extremely small...I *am* sorry for your loss, I truly am, but there is nothing we could have done, and Mrs. Haywood agreed to proceed with the surgery."

My head snapped up, as did the ones of our family.

"WHAT?" my mother screeched, tears streaming down her face. She suddenly looked ten years older than she did a few hours ago. A few hours ago...when we were all home together laughing...

"I spoke directly to her before the surgery. It is my responsibility to tell my patients of their illness, and I..." she took a deep breath, "I told her the chances of her making it through were slim. She said it was alright as long as her baby was safe."

"She knew...she knew..." Was all I could think about...when she spoke to me, and Hayley she knew she was going to...I couldn't even think the words, it hurt too damn much.

"But *you* didn't tell *us*," Riley said.

"No, and again I am sorry about that, but Mrs. Haywood had me promise not to tell you in case she did make it...again I can not tell you how sorry I am," she said, and with one last look of sympathy she turned leaving us to our grief.

How was I suppose to live without my friend, my lover, my wife, my angel...she couldn't be...she was not gone...she was probably going to pop up behind me, scaring the shit out of me like she always did.

"Collin, I'm...gonna take...Hayley home to bed..." my sister tried to tell me. I could barely hear her through her sobs, and the ringing in my ears.

I just nodded, unable to speak. It hurt...it was unbearably painful... how did this happen to us...it was unfair...fourteen months...that was it?

That was all I was permitted...then I lost her...

CHAPTER 32

I rolled over in my bed to stare at the empty space beside me, the same as I'd done every morning for the past ten days, just as I did every night for the past eleven.

If I looked hard enough I could still see her there, smiling at me, that teasing smirk she so often had plastered on her face. How her features contrasted so with the blue sheets, and her porcelain skin. Long black locks falling in her eyes, gently draped along her side as she lay there looking back at me, all wide-eyed, and happy…and her eyes. The way they captured, and enticed my heart; the doors to her soul, the key to mine. Even with my eyes closed I could still see them, a deep emerald green. They glimmered, and glistened even with no light…just like she did, every day.

Her smell lingered still on everything. The bed sheets, the pillows, her books, each room in the house, I could smell her everywhere. Her clothes were still in the closet, and still neatly folded in the drawers. Clean, and pressed, and permeating the room with her sweet aroma.

I didn't want to touch anything of hers in case my own scent washed it out. I didn't want to wake up, and no longer smell her, no longer feel her presence. I was still grasping onto straws I knew I'd eventually have to cut. Ten days later, and I didn't know when I'd ever stop…if I'd ever be able to stop.

I don't think anything could have prepared me for the shear pain my heart went through…was still going through. Nothing could have prepared me for that… emptiness, every fiber of my being ached to be near her, to touch her, to feel her, just to speak to her, tell her how much I loved her…just one last time. How I'd give up anything to just be able to tell her just one last time how much I loved her.

The door creaked open as I looked intently at the pillow, the light from the hallway filtering into the room.

"Daddy?" I heard a pair of small feet padding over to my bed. I looked away from the image of my angel I had projected onto the place next to me, to the smaller, shadowed version slowly making her way over.

I sat up, and smiled at her, "Hey princess. How come you're not in bed?" I asked her; instead of answering right away she crawled up the bed to where I was sitting, and buried her head into my side. Sitting on the side next to the empty space where the covers were cold, but not *in* the empty space. *No one* ever sat in it.

"I couldn't sleep. I had a bad dweam," she said quietly as I cradled her in my arms. I didn't realize until she was gone that I was totally dependent on her. I needed her hand to hold, and it wasn't there. I was so lost. How was I supposed to do this without her?

"I miss mommy," the little girl sniffled as I began stroking her blond curly hair. I felt a lump pull up in my throat as I began stroking it; soft, and long, just like B's had been, just lighter.

"So do I sweetie…I miss her a lot," 'A lot' was more than an understatement.

"I can smell mommy in hewe," Hayley sniffed, and I had to smile a little because it really wasn't just me who could smell her everywhere. It was funny how, now that she was gone, we all longed for anything that reminded us of her. There had been a time where her smell had started an argument with my sister.

"*Well I'm sorry but it looked like one of mine!*" B had laughed while waving a pink t-shirt around.

"*B, since when did you have a shirt that looks like that? In that size? Ever? You don't!*" Mika hadn't been as amused; you do not, and I repeat, do not mess with her designer clothes…and B knew that.

"*Well, I don't know, things go funny in the wash sometimes, easy mistake to make. Here, take it if you want it back.*"

Mika had narrowed her blue eyes, and glared at her before huffing, and folding her arms in defeat. Mika's dryer had broken, and she brought her laundry over the day before.

"*I don't want it now,*" she grumbled, "*It smells like you, and since you were wearing it, you stretched it. You can keep it.*"

"*Aww… c'mon, you sure? I thought you loved how I smell?*" she'd cooed, squishing my sister's cheeks together. She always took to pissing off Mika, and her 'I'm-such-a-fashionnista-can't-stand-how-you-dress' attitude. She did everything, and anything she could to wine her up, and every single time she'd get really pissy, and we were just waiting for her to explode, and then… nothing. She always forgave her, ignored her, and told her she was right and just walked away.

"*B… stop.*" she whined.

"*Go on, say it, you love my smell. C'mon, take a whiff.*" B said teasingly extending her neck to my sister.

"*God you are so weird, I don't love your smell! Go away, and screw your husband,*" she tried swatting her away while B threw herself onto her, and hugged her with all her might careful of her growing stomach.

Mika took the top back a couple of days ago. She had moved in temporarily with me, helping care for Hayley, and Josh. I saw her little pixie self trudging back to the guest room with it in her hands as I came up the stairs.

At first I got a little panicky that maybe she'd moved something I didn't want to be moved, that things wouldn't be how *she* had left them. But everything was exactly the same. All the things on her dresser hadn't moved an inch; I opened the drawers to see everything just as she'd left it. Everything perfect until a tear I hadn't been aware of slid down my face, and dripped onto the blue summer dress neatly folded at the top.

I took it out into my hands as if it would disintegrate if I held it too hard. I sat on the end of our bed for two hours with that dress held to my nose as I inhaled the fabric, my tears soaking into it. I couldn't let go. I knew my B; she'd make it forever if she wanted. She was strong, the strongest person I knew. She had lived through so much shit to prove it a hundred times over.

The one person I'd chosen to spend my life with, and I couldn't have chosen anyone better. She made the past year what it was, she pushed me to do things I never would have done, to love like I never thought possible, and for that I will be eternally grateful. She got me out of my bubble of misery quicker than anyone else, and made me want to be a better man, for her, for Hayley, and now for Josh.

Hayley sat with me until she fell asleep. I gently lifted her, took her back to her room placing her down on her bed. I kissed her forehead, leaving the little lamp light on and the door slightly ajar, just how she liked it. Returning back to my room, I noticed the glow coming from under Josh's door. It was two in the morning, and I knew it was not his feeding time.

I slowly peeked inside before entering to see Mika sitting on the rocking chair B had fallen in love with when we were shopping for the nursery furniture. I leant on the doorframe for a while, my arms crossed over my chest as I watched her.

She caught sight of me standing at the door way, and reached up to wipe the trail of tears on her cheeks.

"You should probably be getting to bed you know. Josh won't wake up for another two hours," I whispered, straightening myself up.

"Yeah... I guess," she spoke quietly, and looked at the crib, sighing, and standing to lean over it. I looked around the room, just like Hayley had asked there were trucks, and cars every where, with stuffed animals, and even princess stuff. The room had no theme what so ever, Hayley just chose a bunch of things to put in there, and shared some of hers. She loved her little brother like no other…and then I saw the pink shirt, hanging on the outside of his closet. I stared at it for a while only being brought back to reality by Mika's voice.

"It gets easier, right?" she asked. I turned my head to see her staring at the shirt as well.

"Yeah, it will. In time…I guess, but we're going to be alright," I said. She wiped her eyes with the back of her hand quickly, and nodded.

When I looked at Josh, when *we* looked at Josh, everyone agreed he was the spitting image of his mother. He had her hair, her eyes, her nose, and my features. But Josh was B.

"Get some sleep, you look tired, and if you need to talk about anything, well, you know where I am right?" she asked of me. I knew I could talk to her whenever, I just couldn't, not now, but it was nice to know I had someone. I knew if I didn't have my family around, I would have been crushed by all of this. I still felt like I was barely hanging on and that was after hours upon hours of time spent talking to my sister, Riley, and my parents. They were all crushed.

"Thanks..." I nodded, and edged out of the room. She followed shutting the door behind her making her way back to her own room, and I stood in the dark hallway.

I couldn't go back to my bed. Not when she wasn't there. Through the day time I could distract myself, other things needed to be done, I had to make plans for the funeral, the kids, my work, life went on. But at night, in the moments that were just ours, when our barriers came down, then I just felt lonely. I felt lonely, I felt empty, and it really hurt. It caused me physical pain, returning to an empty cold bed, expecting my love, my Angel, and finding nothing. It made my chest constrict, it made my stomach sink to the point where I felt sick.

I tried to keep a wall in front of our children, I didn't want to put a downer on the whole family, but at the same time, we were a team. When we realized she was really gone we felt like we were losing the stitching that kept us so nicely blanketed together. B was the stitching, without her we were still together but we were fraying at the edges.

I went back to our room, and on the way I looked at our family pictures on the walls. I noticed the one from last Christmas at my parent's house. We were all there, my parents, Mika, Riley, Hayley, and even Josh; though B was not pregnant by much if you looked carefully you could tell there was a little bump there. All around the picture B had scribbled, '*I love you all forever, and ever, and ever. For always, and then a bit longer. But no more than that, I have things to do, like keeping an eye on all of you trouble makers...*"

I looked at it, and smiled, all of it written unmistakably in Belladonna Haywood's handwriting. I knew it anywhere, it was horrible, and I told her every time she wrote something down, which was a lot of the time. She had many talents; this was not one of them.

"Well I'm so sorry but I'm a psychologist not a calligraphist, and anyway, you don't seem to care too much about my hands when they're on your dick, do you? No. So shut up," she'd say every time I made a snarky comment.

I begrudgingly went back to bed, and layed down closing my eyes. I couldn't help thinking about the last time I had spoken to her, just before they wheeled her into surgery. She knew she wasn't going to make it, and now I remembered her words in a whole new way.

"Angel, you'll be alright. Stop worrying, you'll get better, and we'll go home with our baby boy, Hayley, and you can go back to annoying the shit out of Mika," I said with a shaky voice. *She chuckled.*

"Collin, please let me say this…" she took a deep breath, and closed her eyes for a few seconds before going on, *"You are the best husband I could have hoped for…the best friend, the best father. I seriously could not imagine being with anyone else but you. I'm not leaving you; I'm not ever leaving you. I'm always in your heart, and I love you more than words can describe,"* she whispered weakly.

I did answer her back that I loved her, but I didn't think much of it. She knew she was leaving us. I held the blankets tightly within my fingers, and stared at the wall for what seemed like hours.

I watched as the light slowly crept on the floor until it landed in *her* spot, the sun warming up the cold of her absence. I put my hand to my cheek, and noticed I was crying.

I was seeing it now, thinking of her last words to me, the bigger picture. B was still in it, and she always would be, and we were going to be fine because we were us. We were a family, and we always made it through.

EPILOGUE

Thirteen years later

Fiorello H Laguardia High School of Music…
The stadium was nearly filled one hour before the graduation ceremony was scheduled to begin. I looked across the agora, and couldn't help but smile at the sea of happy faces. Graduation was a time to celebrate the past, and focus on the future. As our family settled into there seats, I focused on their faces, and the past thirteen years of our lives.

Josh was now thirteen years old. He would be a freshman at some Tech school next year. He was a good looking kid considering he looked exactly like his mother. You could see Haywood in his brownish hair, and masculine features. The black of his hair had fated away as a baby, but it was still dark enough to remind me of *her*… my beautiful wife.

Sitting next to the boy were his grandparents, his Aunt Mika, and Uncle Riley. After years of trying, Mika, and Riley were nearly eight months along with their first child. I never would have thought they would end up getting married those two, but hey, what did I know.

"You know how women swoon that bullshit that they just *love* being pregnant. Well, they're all liars. Who could possibly enjoy this? Having to pee all the time, the belly, the bitchiness…" Mika said looking at our mother with annoyance when she started rubbing her belly, and cooing to it.

I almost reminded her that the bitchiness was quintessential Mika, and

189

"She taught me that flowers come in all different colors, that it was okay to be different…." Hayley murmured softly.

She had been four years old when we went to the flower shop, and bought her mother a yellow rose. How could she possibly have remembered that? I grinned wistfully, and squeezed my sister's hand again.

"I miss you mom, and I love you…" Hayley whispered, "Thank you."

The stadium exploded with thunderous applause, well except our family's row. We were too busy weeping into our fucking tissues.

Our tears finally subsided as the ceremony continued. We watched as Hayley, and her friends accepted their diplomas. I noticed she was still holding the yellow flower. We furiously snapped pictures as she made her way back to her seat, and the stadium erupted into cheers as the Class of 2024 threw their caps into the air.

After the recessional, our family was huddled at the east entrance of the stadium waiting for Hayley.

She finally made her way to us, and she hugged us all. We asked another proud parent to snap a family picture of us. As I stood there, waiting for the flash, I couldn't help thinking how much B would have wanted to be here, how much *I* wanted her to be here.

"Remember," I reminded her, "Family dinner's at 5:00."

"I'll be there," she grinned as her buddies tried to pull her away, "Oh, I almost forgot," Hayley rushed to my side, and pulled me into a tight hug, "This is for you."

She handed me the yellow rose, and a card.

I just looked at her with a puzzled look. Hayley smiled, and she gave me a peck on the cheek before rushing toward her huge red Jeep already full of smiling, happy seniors.

As our family made our way to the parking lot, Mika agreed to take Josh with her, and greet everyone at my house for the graduation celebration. I had one stop to make on the way home, and wanted to be alone.

I drove in silence buried within my thoughts. I parked the Mercedes close to the grave site when I arrived at the cemetery, and made my way to *her*. Kneeling down in front of her tomb I cleaned the debris, threw out the old lavender roses, and placed new ones along with the yellow rose from Hayley. I leaned my back against the block with the stone angel on top of it, looking down on me with her impressive wings tucked against her back.

"It's a beautiful day today Angel, the kind of day you liked. Not too cold with the sun shining brightly." I smiled, remembering how her green eyes would shine with the glow of the sun light. After all these years, I haven't forgotten her face, her eyes, her smile or her smell. I made myself remember her, I never wanted to forget.

"You should have seen…let me re-phrase that, I'm sure you *saw* how our little girl rocked her speech in front of the whole school. I'm so proud of her, everyone is. She's smart just like you and I know she'll do great things in this world." I swallowed again, but I didn't hold it in…I let the tears fall freely.

With trembling hands, I carefully unfolded the card Hayley gave me.

You helped me grow, prosper, and reach great heights
When I can't find my way out, you are the one to show me the way
When I cry, so do you, though it brings me no comfort
Even when I'm gone, and on my own, I can always call you
And when you leave this earth to a better place
I will still be a daddy's little princess
Your daughter,
Hayley